Praise for Lucienne Diver's
Bad Blood

"*Bad Blood* is a delightful urban fantasy, a clever mix of Janet Evanovich and Rick Riordan, and a true Lucienne Diver original."

~ *Long and Short Reviews*

"*Bad Blood* is a wonderful read. The mystery keeps the reader engaged, the action makes the reader want to roll with the punches, and the romance makes the senses tingle. This is a great book to coil up with on a lazy Sunday afternoon."

~ *Fresh Fiction*

"...a most pleasant pick-me-up read."

~ *Mrs. Giggles*

Bad Blood

Lucienne Diver

SAMHAIN
PUBLISHING

Samhain Publishing, Ltd.
11821 Mason Montgomery Road, 4B
Cincinnati, OH 45249
www.samhainpublishing.com

Bad Blood
Copyright © 2012 by Lucienne Diver
Print ISBN: 978-1-60928-594-4
Digital ISBN: 978-1-60928-492-3

Editing by Tera Kleinfelter
Cover by Kanaxa

First Samhain Publishing, Ltd. electronic publication: June 2011
First Samhain Publishing, Ltd. print publication: May 2012

Dedication

To my husband, Peter Wheeler, who teases me that I never mention him by name, but who's part of every hero I write.

Acknowledgments

There are so many wonderful people I want to thank for making this book a reality. First and foremost, I want to thank Jennifer Skully/Jasmine Haynes, who accompanied me on our Thelma and Louise-esque trip out to Los Angeles to research the setting of this book, and the amazing Mark Viniello, artist extraordinaire, who showed us around various production design studios. I wish I'd had occasion to use more of what we learned in the book, because it was all so incredible. I also want to thank the uber-talented people at Tatopoulos Studios and Schell Sculpture Studio for giving us a glimpse behind the scenes.

Huge thanks to Tera Kleinfelter for loving BAD BLOOD and for being such a wonderful editor and advocate, everyone at Samhain who had a hand in this book, my agent Kristin Nelson for believing, and my family for constant support and inspiration. A crazy cast of characters like my heroine's cadre doesn't come out of nowhere!

Chapter One

"Stake-out: a mind-numbing, bladder-busting exercise distinguishable from stalking by the ID you're able to flash when the police come tap-tap-tapping at your Camaro door."

—Tori Karacis, Karacis Investigations

I needed a shrink and a ladies' room—not necessarily in that order. I was still new enough to early mornings spent staring at storefronts to have downed a double espresso without considering the consequences. Not so long ago I'd left the circus to join Uncle Christos, the *other* black sheep of the family, in his PI business. More recently he'd run off to find himself, having taught me everything I know, which is, unfortunately, not everything *he* knew. And so I came to be muddling through my first solo stake-out, seriously questioning my sanity, not to mention my stick-to-it-iveness.

Not that this was a stake-out exactly.

Okay, I *was* illegally parked near a hydrant watching my quarry disorder the staff at Renee's by showing up a half hour late for her nail appointment and, it appeared, expecting instant service. As soon as she was captive to her wet nails I'd be on the move, springing to present her with my client's proposal. If I could wait that long. If only she'd been on time, I wouldn't be in such dire straits.

Circe, high-powered Hollywood agent—and nigh-immortal enchantress, at least according to my eccentric grandmother—was *not* an easy person to pin down. No amount of charm or subterfuge had gotten me past her legion of hangers-on. 'Course, I never had accepted defeat easily.

I'd chosen my target—one of Circe's administrative assistants whose shoes seemed a little less spit-shined, whose hair had a tendency to frizz as though she couldn't afford the really high-end shellac that served the others—and culled her from the herd. Okay, so I'd followed her to the ladies' room and bribed her with a good chunk of my retainer, but it had bought me Circe's schedule for the day.

Finally, Circe chose a clichéd blood red and turned herself over to the manicurist. I waited until her delicate digits were soaking in some solution before sauntering into Renee's as casually as possible, sweeping a speculative eye over the displays as if I were an interested customer, and heading for the restroom.

Circe didn't know me from Adam—or anyway, Eve—as I'd not been able to get within spitting distance yesterday. Dressed in one of those spiffy black work-out suits with racing stripes matching the hot pink sports bra underneath, I blended in with ninety percent of the women in L.A.—actresses, aspiring or otherwise, running to and from the gym, and the fitness professionals who catered to them. Nothing about me should have raised a red flag. It should have been safe enough. And yet...

When I emerged from the bathroom a minute later, Circe's seat was empty and the back exit was closing with a soft snick.

I didn't know what had spooked Circe—surely not me!—but I wasn't about to lose her now.

I bolted for the exit, cursing as I ran. The one minion Circe'd brought along headed to intercept, but I froze him with a look. Not enough gorgon in my blood to turn man or woman to stone, only enough to give them pause. Or, as I chose to believe, the family tales were hokum and I was just that scary.

I couldn't have been more than seconds behind Circe, but they'd been crucial. When I burst out into the alley, Circe was already fighting for her life, backed up against a rusted-out dumpster, clawing at the hands that gripped her. Her assailant looked like something straight off Hollywood Boulevard, dressed like a famous screen character come to life to gouge tips from photo-mad tourists. A brown fedora was pulled low and his trench coat collar raised high to shadow his face—Mike Hammer, maybe, or some other hardboiled PI gone over to the dark side. Something was wrong with the hand bruising Circe's throat, but there was no time for analysis. I was far more concerned with the hand I couldn't see, the one that thrust into Circe's chest, unleashing a tide of blood to spill over his cuff and down her silk shirt.

The salon door flew open as I launched myself at the grappling pair. Behind me, Circe's minion yelled, his cry cut off a second later as the attacker's head whipped around and a gale-force wind arose from nowhere to hurl me into him. Pain blossomed across my back as I hit the rock-solid body at speed then exploded as we crashed to a sudden stop against the wall. The alley rang with the sharp crack of the minion's head against the brick face. I landed atop him in a tangle of body parts and twisted my head enough to see that he still breathed, but it was all the time I could spare from Circe. Already her body had gone limp and the light in her eyes was flickering out.

I fought the pain as I gathered my legs beneath me for another offensive. The attacker was distracted with the effort to free his hand from Circe's chest cavity. I swallowed the bile burning up my throat and flew into action, closing the distance just in time to watch Circe fall to the ground, the gaping hole in her chest leaking gore and an equally noxious liquid starting to seep through her skirt.

I grabbed the arm of her assailant—killer—as he turned to run and froze as my brain suddenly registered what I was now seeing close up. The hands were scaly, clawed and blue-green. He turned on me with a look of malicious madness, ran his tongue over teeth that were again simply wrong and wrenched himself out of my grip.

He was gone in the second it took me to get a hold of myself. I was torn between pursuit and seeing to the victims. I wish I could have been certain that I chose the latter out of something more noble than fear, but I couldn't. My faculties were falling all over themselves trying to come up with some plausible denial for what I'd seen.

A choked-off cry from the direction of Renee's spun me around. Several women had appeared at the back door, jockeying for a position that allowed maximum viewing with minimum exposure. The pack leader actually squeaked as my gaze, probably still feral, met hers.

"W-we've called 9-1-1," she said, as if in threat.

"Good," I answered, consciously relaxing my body posture even though I felt anything but relaxed.

I wondered when they'd appeared and what they'd made of what they'd seen. Hopefully enough to cast me in the right role—would-be rescuer rather than psychopath. Unfortunately, there was no telling what mental aerobics their brains, like mine, would perform to account for the inconceivable. Most people had no context for Mickey Spillane meets Creature from the Black Lagoon. Hell, I came from a long line of circus freaks—literally—and *I* had no context. *Illiad*, *Odyssey*, and centuries of cultural and family history aside, I still couldn't wrap my mind around it.

Slowly, so as not to spook anyone, I adjusted my disheveled sweat suit and approached the minion, who was still slumped against the building's blackened brick face. I willed him to live, not only for the obvious humanitarian reasons, but because he was my best hope. As one of Circe's adherents, chances were he'd seen the unexplained enough that fish-face's appearance wouldn't have thrown him for a loop. If I had to explain to the police that I'd fought off an oversized misfit with a skin condition, I wanted backup. The police still weren't too happy with me over the Cruikshank affair.

Luckily, the minion moaned and started to stir upon my approach, though his eyes, when they opened, wouldn't focus. Concussion then, at the very least.

"Ambulance on the way?" I called to the gaggle in the doorway.

The woman who'd answered before nodded. "*And police.*"

Clearly, I hadn't made her hit parade.

I pushed down on the minion as he started to rise. "Don't move," I suggested firmly, hitting him with the full force of my stare. The fact that he subsided could have been sheer coincidence. I was tempted to collapse right down beside him now that my adrenaline rush was wearing off and my muscles were going shaky on me, but checked the impulse. First, the alley was ripe with the acquired grime of lifetimes going tacky in the rising heat and redolent of sour milk and the sickly sweet smell of death. Second, while this job was caput, since there was no possible way short of a trip across the river Styx of presenting my client's proposal to the dragon lady, I was an inveterate snoop and there was sleuthing to be done.

Still moving slowly, hands in plain sight of my audience so that I couldn't possibly be accused of tampering with evidence, I turned to survey the scene. It took a minute to look beyond the all-too-human expression on Circe's face—shock mixed with irritation, as if death was a wrinkle she didn't have time for—and note the details.

The dragon lady would have been horrified to see herself, head cocked at an unnatural angle by the dumpster she wouldn't in life have touched with someone else's ten-foot pole, legs splayed, skirt of her power suit riding up nearly to her waist, chest pried open, broken ribs poking through the gaping hole. Irreverently, I marveled that a missing heart would put down a Hollywood agent. I'd thought that came standard.

I checked my brain before it could babble on along those lines and forced myself to keep processing the scene. I'd just about kill—damn, bad wording—to get a look at the briefcase that had slid halfway across the alley to rest in what appeared to be a puddle of motor oil. In the time I'd watched Circe, waiting for my moment, it had never left her side. She used it to body-check persistent supplicants who managed to get too close, stop doors from closing when a hanger-on failed to anticipate her need and, presumably, kept her secrets within. If I wanted access, I was going to have to play nicely with the boys in blue.

Detective Nick Armani—no relation—tried to stare me down from the other side of the tiny vanity table *cum* desk in Renee's office, which had been temporarily appropriated. He was tall, dark and none too happy to see me. I had to admit the glower was effective, with those brows in desperate need of taming lowered to shade pale blue eyes. I didn't think he'd be gratified to find that the effect on me was anything but intimidating, especially with his knees bumping the girly desk every time he shifted. It should have been comical—probably would have been if I weren't still having flashbacks to the wet sound of the fishman yanking his hand from Circe's chest—but it also emphasized his fairly impressive proportions.

"Tori Karacis," he said, just as the silence was starting to get interesting. "Why is it that I always seem to find you at my crime scenes?"

"*Yours*, detective? Do you have something to confess? I'd be glad to make a citizen's arrest, especially if you'll let me borrow your cuffs."

Damn. My brain and mouth always seemed to disconnect in the detective's presence. No wonder he glowered.

And yet, I thought I might almost have detected a twitch of the lips. Play nice, I reminded myself.

"No such luck," he answered, rocking backwards on Renee's spindly chair. "If there's any restraining to be done—"

The office door opened, interrupting whatever he'd been about to say—and dammit, I wanted to *hear*. No surprise the impeccable timing had been brought to us by none other than Armani's esteemed partner Detective Helen Lau, who from our first meeting acted as though she'd despise me if only she could work up that much enthusiasm.

"I've got Officer Jennings doing a ride-along in the ambulance with the male vic. We're still waiting on the ME. Learned anything so far?" she asked.

I couldn't help myself. "You're just in time. Detective Armani was about to break out the rubber hoses."

Lau finally deigned to look my way, but couldn't be moved to put on an expression, let alone respond. Damn, I wanted to rattle her cage. This whole *more stoic than thou* thing—and *hello*, I wasn't even in competition—freaked me out. Of course, that might have been why she did it.

Armani gave me a quelling look, but I'd had years of Yiayia's evil eye to draw on. I was nigh unquellable.

"Actually," he said, heading things off before they could get ugly, "Tori was just about to volunteer what she knows. We're good here. Why don't you begin on the customers so they can be released? You might want to start on the one with the really piercing voice so we can all hear ourselves think."

Lau's eyes flickered to me and back to Armani before she nodded. "Call if you need me."

He nodded back and again we had the room to ourselves.

Sighing heavily, he thumped the dainty chair back down onto four legs, dropped his elbows onto the surface of the desk and began rubbing his temples. He speared me with a look as I shifted on my own chair.

"Why do you do that?" he asked.

I shrugged. "She makes me crazy."

"What do you mean *makes*?"

I watched him rub his temples. I knew a killer pressure-point hand massage that would clear that headache right up, but even if I were foolish enough to offer it, the thought of Detective Lau walking in on such a scene would put the kibosh on the temptation.

"Anyway," I continued, ready to cut him some slack, "you wanted to know everything, right?"

His head came up out of his hands. "Just like that?"

"Well, *now* you're expecting the smart-ass comments. I don't want to be predictable."

He eyed me suspiciously. "Fair enough. Mind if I record?"

"Knock yourself out."

Armani drew a mini-cassette recorder from his inside jacket pocket, gave the details on the interview, asked me to state my name and set it down between us.

I gave him the whole song and dance, blushing a bit as I 'fessed up to the pit stop, and ending with the getaway. Unfortunately, Armani picked right up on the details that were glossed over along the way.

"I don't understand. If the killer was busy with the vic, how did he manage to knock you back against the wall?"

Damn, the man was too sharp. "I don't know—had to be something in his hand."

"Like what?"

"Hell if I know, I was too busy flying through the air."

"Okay, we'll come back to that. Your client's proposal—you have it on you?"

"Yes."

"Can I see it?"

I weighed the pros of cooperating with authorities against the cons of invading my client's privacy. "Not unless you've got a warrant."

"How can I have a warrant when I didn't know a damned thing about it until just now?"

I took that as a rhetorical question.

His glower was back. "Do you have something to hide?"

"'Not I,' said the cat. My client's another matter. Whatever he had to say to Circe was private. For her eyes only. Even I don't know what's in the envelope."

"You didn't sneak a peek?"

"It's sealed."

"Seals can be broken."

I gave him Yiayia's fish-eye, which he ignored. "Remind me never to ask you to pick up my mail. Anyway, I'm not a snoop."

Armani quirked an eyebrow at me.

"Not *that* kind of snoop anyway," I huffed.

"So you only invade people's privacy for money."

Okay, that was uncalled for. And totally untrue. Truth was I only respected privacy when bound by confidentiality or the laws of California. I couldn't speak to what curiosity had done to the cat, but I did know what it had done to my familial relationships. I'd also learned through painful experience that the truth wasn't likely to set us free. Sometimes it was about as welcome as a cockroach in the soup. It was one of the reasons— beyond the debilitating fear of heights that kept me out of the family acrobatic act—that the Rialto Brothers Circus had been just as happy to see the back of me as I'd been to split.

I shoved those oh-so-happy thoughts back into their little black box. "Something like that."

"We can subpoena your records."

"Uh huh," I answered, unconcerned. Since I hadn't completed the job, there was no report on file for the client. There'd been no notes to take and I'd be giving the envelope back to my client as soon as possible. "So then I'm free to go?"

"As long as you come by the station later to sign your statement and look at mug shots."

There was no good way to tell him that would be an exercise in futility. Still, later sounded sufficiently vague.

"Later then," I answered, already halfway to the door.

Armani let me go, but I could feel his eyes on me all the way out. I was tempted to peel off the jacket to give him a real show, my sports bra ending well above the waistline of the pants, but the envelope sat in the special inside pocket of the jacket and I wasn't sure I was smooth enough not to send it flying. Besides, I wasn't all that certain to be a crowd-pleaser. A shortly thereafter *ex*-boyfriend had once described me as "good enough for television", which in this town was a slap in the face. It meant that with my unruly black hair, dark eyes and slight build, I probably wouldn't break the camera but neither would I carry a show on the big screen.

Unless, of course, it was the sideshow I'd just embroiled myself in.

Chapter Two

"Sometimes when you look a gift-horse in the mouth you get bit—and sometimes you get that green slobber all over your hands that comes from them eating grass all day. I'm not saying don't do it. Just be prepared."

—Uncle Christos

There was nothing I wanted more than to find a highway and *drive*, fast and furious. Not that I could outrace my thoughts, but having every last wit focused on hazards and speed traps ought to put them on hold—at least until the near-death experience of the whole thing snapped them into perspective. Unfortunately, I'd mistimed my escape to coincide with rush hour. The slow crawl was enough to drive me out of my mind.

By the time I reached my office, I was literally shaking—arms, legs, hell, brain cells all doing the jitterbug. Shock had set in or maybe worn off. Had I really just been all flippant with the police practically over Circe's dead body? What the hell was wrong with me? I'd heard of gallows humor, but this was the first time I'd participated—assuming that anything I'd said could remotely be accounted humorous.

Jesus (ironically pronounced "Hey-Zeus" and, again, no relation), the part-time assistant I'd inherited from my uncle along with the fichus, the caseload and the rent on a second-floor office in a historic building downtown, was gone by the time I arrived. Uncle Christos had described the place as charming—and it was, if charming meant cracked tiles in the entryway, cracked paint on the walls and nary a closet. I couldn't help but think that any one of those noir detectives whose exploits I'd devoured in my youth—Marlowe, Archer, Hammer, Spade—would have been at home in the seedy surroundings.

On the upside, we had high ceilings, honest-to-God moldings and warmly painted walls that I called buttermilk, but that Jesus assured me was "crème anglaise". Since Jesus, as the only one who understood our filing system, was the keeper of all knowledge, it wasn't wise to cross him. I let him have his little victory. The sepia-tone pictures of old L.A. Uncle Christos had spaced around the office added class, but did nothing to liven the place up.

Just to thumb my nose at all the gravitas, I'd added touches to my own office, like the singing fish mounted above my door, which for sanity's sake I'd removed the batteries from within a week. I'd also strung chili-pepper lights above my windows for the pleasingly tacky effect. There didn't seem to be any good place for fuzzy dice.

It was going on three months since Uncle had bolted for parts unknown, leaving the whole kit and caboodle—somehow the place made me think in words like that—in my lap. The winds of change, not to mention an actual color palette, were due to blow through at any moment. Must and dust and gravitas were not my bag. There had to be a way to mod the place up on a budget and still impress the clients. I'd just been too busy to take matters in hand.

I headed straight for the coffeemaker in the kitchenette off Uncle's office and busied myself with getting a pot started, psyching myself up to dash my client's hopes and dreams. It wasn't that I wussed out over delivering bad news—that was an occupational hazard—more that it was his case that had put me face-to-face with a killer and I was in no mood for an argument over whether or not I'd earned my fee. The retainer was non-refundable, said so right in the contract, but when the chips were down, the haggling would commence and any balances due were hell to collect.

Five minutes later I was playing Freecell on my computer, not as a stalling technique—perish the thought—just as something to do while I got a bit more caffeine into my system and gathered my thoughts. But my concentration was shot all to hell and after being stumped two games in a row, I had to admit defeat or further blow my statistics. Sighing, I closed down the game and opened my Rolodex.

Kasim King answered on the very first ring, making me wonder whether Circe's death had already hit the news or whether he was just anxious for her reply.

"Mr. King?" I asked, just to be sure.

"Speaking. Ms. Karacis?"

He'd heard my voice once, two days ago when he hired me. Either he was, as I suspected, waiting for my call or he had a good ear for voices even when distorted over phone lines.

"That's me. Have you heard the news yet?"

A beat, and then, "What news?"

"Mr. King, I'm afraid I was unable to present your proposal to Ms. Holland. She was killed today."

"Killed? She's *dead*?"

I'd expected dejection, resignation maybe, but not wonder and even, maybe, *hope*.

Puzzled, I answered, "Yes, sadly, I can confirm that personally. Would you like me to return your proposal or is there someone else at her company you'd like me to approach?"

Circe, it was well-known, had clung tightly to the reins of her talent agency, never letting anyone else's star shine brightly enough to wash out her own, but there'd been rumors recently of a partnership—all very wink, wink, nudge, nudge in the trade magazines Jesus left around the office.

"Circe's *dead*?" he repeated, as if still trying to wrap his mind around it. "I'll be damned. I didn't know it was even possible."

"Mr. King?"

"Sorry. Sorry, I was just—thinking. Well, I guess that changes everything. No need to return the envelope. Just, I don't know, burn it. Shred it. Whatever."

O-kay, I thought. "There's one more thing," I continued, hating to kill the odd relief Circe's death seemed to have inspired, "since I was on the scene, the police may be interested in the case that brought me there. Unless you want to come forward, I'll continue to keep things confidential until I'm hit with a warrant."

Another beat. "Thanks for the warning. How about I come by and relieve you of that envelope and you do whatever else you have to do?"

Definite caution there. Curiouser and curiouser. I'd assumed the envelope contained pages from a screenplay or maybe headshots—though given Mr. King's apparent age and, er, weathered condition, my money was on the former— certainly nothing that needed to be burned, shredded or kept from the police. Maybe King was paranoid, though that wouldn't explain his strange reaction to Circe's death. Then there was that odd comment about how he "didn't know it was possible". A million questions vied for attention, but none that I could focus on if I expected to keep up my end of the conversation.

"That sounds fine. When would you like to come by?"

"How about now?"

"I'm just on my way out," I found myself saying. "Tomorrow would be better."

"What time do you open?"

After I'd hung up, I pulled the envelope from inside my jacket pocket and sat it on the desk in front of me. Somewhere along the line, my subconscious, knowing that my conscious would object, had taken Armani's words "seals can be broken" straight to heart. I picked up the envelope again for study—sturdy, manila, a bit mangled from the alleyway scuffle, sealed solely by the gummy backing. Not exactly high security; easy enough to open and reclose with no one the wiser.

I struggled with myself. On the one hand, the contents could have nothing to do with Circe's murder—which nobody was paying me to investigate in any case. King was clearly surprised to hear of the death and didn't even pretend to sorrow, which surely he would have done had he been guilty, unless he was being far too clever. On the other hand, there was that whole curiosity thing. Was I actually capable of turning the envelope over to King without looking inside?

I tabled the question in favor of another. Could King really believe that Circe was *the* Circe of myth and legend? It would explain the surprise about her death, but *come on*. I mean, sure, I'd flippantly thought of Circe that way, partly based on the infectious ravings of my grandmother, who fervently believed the gods walked among us, and partly because the Hollywood scuttlebutt seemed to confirm that whatever Circe was, it was both more and less than human. Still, it seemed about as likely as—well—me truly turning a man to stone. *Or a scaly mutant murderer?* my inner devil's advocate taunted.

Okay, imagining for a moment that we were dealing with *that* Circe, didn't goddess-hood go hand-in-hand with immortality? I racked my brain, wishing I'd humored Yiayia a bit more when she went on and on about the Olympians. If I remembered correctly, pantheonic history, mythology, whatever you wanted to call it, was pretty inconsistent on the invincibility of gods, goddesses and their progeny. The gorgons, supposedly of my own family tree, were sisters born of the same divine mother (Ceto) and father (Phorcys), yet two were immortal and the third, Medusa, inexplicably was not. Come to think of it, Circe's own brother Phaethon had been killed when Zeus struck him down for driving Helios's sun chariot too close to the Earth. So, either there were levels of immortality or all it really meant was that you lived until someone was properly motivated to see you dead.

In that case, the amazing thing was not that Circe had been murdered, but that it had taken so long. Just off the top of my head, I could think of a number of people she'd pissed off, perhaps mortally: Odysseus, who she'd held for over a year after turning his men to swine; Penelope, his long-suffering wife; Poseidon or Glaucus, depending on whose "history" you read, because Circe'd turned the beloved nymph Scylla into a multi-headed monster; Scylla herself; even Picus, who she'd morphed into a woodpecker (of all things!). But these grudges were centuries old.

The envelope called to me. I tried to drown it out, searching the Internet for more recent references to Circe. It was fascinating reading. In the now, Circe Holland had been linked to everybody from Michael Eisner to gag-me-with-a-silver-spoon child stars Mary Jo and Katie Mann. Based on the numerous articles that took her name in vain, she'd poached stars from other heavy hitters like CAA and ICM. By all accounts, this was not a woman anyone wanted as an adversary. Her list of enemies read like an L.A. phone book.

I'd fiddled, I'd futzed, but still the envelope called. I knew there was no way short of knockout drops that I'd be sleeping tonight without a peek at the contents. So, I started the coffeemaker up again, this time without grounds, to work up some steam.

In the meanwhile, as penance, I flipped through the Strohmeyer file looking for inspiration. I'd hit a wall in the search for Mrs. S's missing hound, Honey, which had seemingly vanished off the face of the earth around the same time her husband had jumped ship. When she'd come in a week ago bearing a dog carrier and a, pardon the phrase, hangdog expression, I'd been all ready to tell her I didn't do missing pooch cases. Unfortunately, pride didn't cover office expenses. Plus, it might have been just the least bit intriguing that she didn't show any concern over the absent Mr. Strohmeyer and that the carrier was so new it bore the remnants of the sale tag. I wasn't sure how exactly it added up, but that part of me that had devoured Nancy Drew, Nero Wolfe and everything in between smelled a mystery and, as experience had shown, I was constitutionally incapable of walking away.

Only now that I'd run through the retainer was it clear what I'd let myself in for. Dogs didn't leave paper trails—at least not the bureaucratically traceable kind. AWOL husbands who might know their hound's whereabouts were another matter. Or should have been anyway. Only this one refused to be so cooperative. No, he had to be clever and pull a complete Houdini. I was stumped.

I scanned my notes and the photos Mrs. S had supplied, but I just couldn't seem to focus. Still, I knew there was a part of my mind taking it all in. Processing. Maybe this time something would click.

Backbrain whirring like my computer hard drive, I carried the envelope into the kitchenette to check on the building steam. Water filled the carafe and condensation fogged the glass. We were good to go.

I removed the carafe from the machine and sat it on the counter with the top open to release the steam. Then I held the flap of the envelope above the mist—close enough for effect, far enough to keep away the telltale warpage from moisture. Uncle's desk was closer and cleaner than mine, so I set the envelope down on the surface, grabbed his silver letter opener and painfully slowly eased it under the flap. Success!

Now the trick was to disturb the contents as little as possible. I fled back to my office for a pair of gloves and my digital camera, just in case the contents were interesting enough to record for posterity. The gloves, which we bought in bulk, were not the sturdier and more expensive surgical models, but cheap plastic disposables that felt, more or less, like wearing sandwich bags. Prepped now, I regained my seat and gently slid two sheets of paper from the envelope. When I finished reading, I started all over again.

Dear Circe:

Neo Cain here. Excuse the unorthodox communiqué. If only you'd return my calls...but I know how precious your time is, so I'll get right to the point. I have a proposal: my life for my daughter's. Despite all my warnings to her, my daughter Elyssa signed one of your damned contracts. I know that I no longer, thanks to my own stupidity and your persuasion, have my own youth and vitality and so I'll have to offer more to compensate. What I propose is fifteen of my years for ten of Elyssa's. I know I

25

can't appeal to your compassion, so let me appeal to your pocket. This will keep my daughter, your investment, young, beautiful and earning you megabucks longer than under your current agreement.

I couldn't convince her that the Big Break wasn't worth her life, but I can correct that failing if only you'll let me. The paperwork is enclosed, lacking only your signature and whatever voodoo you do to enforce it. You know how to reach me with your decision.

Neo Cain

The big quake could not have caused greater shock. Never in a million years would I have guessed that Kasim King and Neo Cain were one and the same. I mean, he'd seemed a bit familiar, but lord he'd gotten *old*. Could I be reading correctly that Circe was prolonging her life by stealing years from others in exchange for fame and fortune? It boggled the mind. Was it possible that immortality came free, but youth cost? If so, Circe's death could only be a boon to society. Presumably, the drain on Circe's victims would end with her death.

That was an awful lot of motive for murder—salvation or revenge—assuming her victims knew what they were agreeing to. Clearly, Neo Cain had, either before or after the fact. If Circe's contract spelled it out, why wasn't she denounced as a lunatic? Was her success enough for people to sell their lives short for the promise of glitz and adoration? Or was it in the fine print, something unread or easily laughed off as an eccentric delusion?

My camera mocked me from the desktop. There was no point in photographing the letter and attached agreement. Who would I show them to? It might make a good case for my client's insanity should he be implicated, but the police weren't likely to pursue the whole magical angle.

And there it was, the three-hundred-pound gorilla, glaring me in the face and daring me to look away. One wacko client, a few rantings—oh yeah, and a freakish killer—and I was ready to be fitted for my straightjacket and padded cell. *Magic and divinity time-sharing our mundane little world.* A hysterical laugh bubbled up, only to be instantly squelched by lack of air. I gasped, trying to suck oxygen past the sudden vise around my lungs. A panic attack? Me? Surely I was made of sterner stuff. I fought it down, doing my best to clear my head, slow my inhalations.

I'd been so smug all this time, laughing at my family's quirks, humoring Yiayia when she talked about the origin of her beard or the power my mother had to stop men in their tracks or how so many famous people were really gods in disguise come to Hollywood to regain a measure of their former adoration, and here it was...

My natural cynicism reasserted itself. None of this could exactly be called conclusive. My client could be passed off as a madman. Circe's name might be no more than coincidence. And the fish-man? B-movie extra. Sideshow freak—we had several in my family alone. *Yeah, how do you explain being flung into Circe's minion without so much as a touch?* my inner killjoy asked. *Special effect,* I answered defiantly. After all, this was Holly-weird. Probably all this wasn't even abnormal. I'd moved here less than a year ago; it wasn't as if I'd seen all the town had to offer.

It was thin and I knew it, like putting my hands over my ears and la-la-la-ing the nastiness away, but I was able to breathe again. Undoubtedly, there'd be a limited shelf life on my willful ignorance. I needed a serious dose of normalcy to stave off its expiration.

Carefully, I slid the papers back into the envelope and used the lingering steam to moisten the glue so that I could refasten the flap. Then I carried the envelope back to my desk, locked it in the top drawer and reached for the phone to call my best friend, the most normal person I knew, Christie Rostenkowski.

The phone rang just as my hand landed.

"Karacis Investigations," I answered.

"Ohmagod, did you hear?" Christie gushed without so much as a hello. Without waiting for an answer, she continued, "Circe Holland was murdered practically around the corner from me! I literally could have walked right into it. I pass that alley every day. And in broad daylight!"

Christie was like that, phased by all the wrong things, untouched by others. Between her parents' money and her own blonde-hair-blue-eyed supermodel looks, people fell all over themselves to shelter Christie from reality's little speed bumps.

That was, in fact, how we'd met, when I'd backed down two bozos who were hassling her in a pizza parlor. She made me think of Cindy Lou Who. Faced with the Grinch himself, she too would have been mollified by a lame story and a pat on the head. I liked her because it was near impossible not to; she got a kick out of me because I was "like, so totally *yourself*". I never had asked her who else I was supposed to be.

Anyway, she'd paused and needed an answer. "Yeah, I heard."

"*Well*, isn't it awful?" she moaned.

"Did you know her?" Christie was an actress/model of the commercial, catalogue and occasional walk-on variety.

"That's kind of a non sequitur, isn't it? I mean, is it any less awful if I didn't?"

Points for her. "No," I answered, drawing the word out. "I'm just saying that not every death is necessarily a tragedy."

Christie gasped, and I wondered if I shouldn't maybe have kept that thought to myself. Moral ambiguity was probably not a common visitor to her world.

"What I mean is, what if cutting short one life prolonged others?" I realized even as I said it that Circe's scheme had essentially been this in reverse. Was I really on the moral high ground here or had I just argued shades of the same crime?

"You know something," she accused.

Damn, I had to watch myself.

"I was there," I admitted.

Immediately, Christie's voice changed. "Oh, you poor thing. Do you want me to come over? I could bring chocolate or something. I was going to ask if you wanted to come clubbing with me tonight. A friend got me on the list for Ondago's."

I grimaced. "I'd be terrible company tonight. I'm sorry. Rain check?"

"Okay," she said doubtfully, "but when you're up to it, I also wanted to get your opinion on my new head shots."

I'm pretty sure I kept my groan internal. As soon as we'd hung up, I realized that Christie never had answered my question about whether she'd known the dragon lady.

Chapter Three

"Gods, like lima beans, should be avoided at all costs—and if unavoidable, taken in very small doses."
—Avra Spyropoulous, a.k.a. Yiayia

My alarm went off way too damned early Friday morning. Normally, unless I had an appointment, I rolled in somewhere between ten and eleven. Today, though, Neo Cain, alias Kasim King, had said he'd be by first thing for the envelope. I could have let Jesus handle the handoff, but I wanted to—well, in all honesty, I didn't know what. Maybe ask him some questions to watch for his reactions.

After a quick shower, I ran mousse through my hair, scrunched it a bit and let it be. I had only two options with my hair—fuss way too damned long and look like I stepped out of a Clairol commercial or not mess with it at all and get passable, if irrepressible curls. Anything in between, like blow-drying, and I was frizz city.

My wardrobe was pretty much all variations on a theme—black to which splashes of color could be applied via scarves, camisoles or pins. Easy to mix and match. Not feeling at all sporty today, I chose a black pants suit over a periwinkle silk tank with matching scarf and low-heeled boots. Somehow, looking together made me feel more together, like I was putting on my professional persona. World-weary PI. Yup, been there, done that, perfectly unfazed by psycho killers and crazy contracts.

I'd been in my office all of five minutes when Jesus burst in, literally glowing. Jesus didn't glow. He sniffed; he raised eyebrows. At most he looked mildly amused at your expense.

He closed the door behind him and leaned against it for support. "Someone here to see you and all I can say is oh. My. God!"

I was dumbfounded. "Well, who is it?"

"If I find out you've been hiding him from me—"

"*Jesus*, who is it?" I asked again.

"It's Apollo-freakin'-Demas. About a *case*, he says."

Ignoring the lightning bolt of shock that struck me, I opted for infuriatingly calm. "And that's surprising why? We are investigators—at least one of us is."

"Honey, stars like Apollo do not shop downtown for PIs. They have their people call someone else's people who hire some firm at a chichi Hollywood address. They do not appear in person, in the *a.m.*" *As if this was a crime.* "I hear Travolta insists on doing all his business at night, just so he doesn't get mobbed."

Put that way...

"Well, we'll never know what it's about unless you show him in, assuming stars like him wait around. Go. Oh, hold up." I unlocked my desk drawer and handed him the envelope. "If Kasim King shows up, give him this."

Jesus saluted, then turned on his heel and marched sharply out of my office.

I slid my chair back in preparation to rise in greeting, then forgot all about it in the next second when all of a sudden, there he was—Apollo-freakin'-Demas, all six foot two ridiculously ripped inches of him. I had one of those bizarre romantic-comedy moments where the world contracts, spatial relationships are meaningless and he was all there was in the world—just his turquoise eyes meeting my bronze, silently speaking volumes. All those statues carved in his likeness were such pale imitations as to be sacrilege.

Then I shook it off.

"Okay, I *get* it. If I stipulate that you're a hottie, can we cut the act and move on?"

The look on Apollo's face was so worth the price of admission.

"How?" he asked.

He was already rebounding with an intimate smile, but at the same time his gaze sharpened, as if he were suddenly really focused on *me* and not just whatever had brought him in.

I shrugged. "Cynicism. It's a gift."

"And not your only one."

"Oh. You. Charmer," I deadpanned, choosing blatant insincerity over the more overt and somewhat-soggier rudeness of a raspberry.

"You think so?" he asked undaunted.

"Isn't that why you bring in the big bucks?"

"Oh, is *that* why? Nothing at all to do with my talent then," he shot back.

Damn, he was good at the banter. The more I felt myself responding, the more inexplicably irked I became. "I don't think you came to me for a critique. Why don't you take a seat and tell me why you're here."

Apollo grinned, as if he could see right through me. He tugged my distressed leather guest chair into a position more to his liking and didn't so much settle in as take it over. His long legs stretched out before him, his posture relaxed just slightly and his arms curved around the rests. I tried not to notice the way that strained the black silk T-shirt across his pecs or the way the supremely fitted jeans outlined his thighs.

When I dragged my gaze back up to meet his, I was disconcerted to find him studying me the same way. Well, not the same exactly—not like a starved person eyeing filet minon—more like a birder avidly noting the characteristics of some rare or maybe previously undiscovered species.

He seemed in no hurry to begin, so I gave him a prompt. "Why don't I set the scene, get the ball rolling? My assistant tells me that stars like you don't come down from the heavens for mere mortals like me, so I'm guessing this is too confidential to trust to an underling? And, since I'm a little outside your social strata, you probably didn't pick me out of the phone book, so dish."

"Dish?"

I rolled my eyes. Interactions with Armani aside, I wasn't generally this big a pain in the ass. I just had a tendency to give my inner wiseass free rein when something put me off-kilter. It tended to tip the scales back in my favor.

"That's your cue to jump right in, the water's fine."

Apollo cocked his head to one side. His lips quirked and his eyes sparkled in what I took to be—oh holy freakin' moly. He wasn't the least bit put off. He was, gods help me, intrigued. The old tales had more than enough warnings about what happened to mortals naïve enough to play with gods. I had no urge to become immortalized as a flower, tree or monster. Not that he was, of course, a god. The whole thing was just silly.

Even if those azure eyes, the red-gold hair, the sun-kissed warmth of...

Apollo settled back into his chair and rolled his shoulders, drawing my eyes to that fantastically sculpted chest, which nicely matched the washboard abs below. He crossed one ankle over the other knee; the denim looked soft to the touch, as if—I became aware of two things: one, I hadn't blinked in a while, and two, Apollo knew *exactly* what he was doing.

I cleared my throat and pointedly brought my gaze back up to meet his. I didn't think my look was any too warm, but he didn't seem likely to catch cold.

"Very well," he said finally, "I'm here about Circe Holland."

He paused for my reaction, but, receiving none, since I'd already figured as much, went on. "I understand you've started an investigation into her death."

Suspicion niggled at me. "*Really?* And where are you getting your information, the Delphic Oracle?"

He registered surprise that I'd made the connection. "Psychic to the Stars," he admitted. "And before you ask, not *that* Network. They gave us all a bad name. Anyway, if you don't already have a client, I'd like to hire you to track down the killer."

I shouldn't have been so flummoxed. Certainly, it didn't speak volumes for my competence as an investigator. I'd expected to be questioned, maybe, because the police had let my name slip and Apollo wanted to hear about Circe's final moments. I hadn't expected to be hired if I so chose. Hard as it was to refuse a "god", that was by no means a given. On the one hand, a successful case for Apollo might give me an entrée into L.A. high society and real money, which for an office on a shoestring budget was nothing to sneeze at. On another, it meant getting entangled with beings orders of magnitude beyond my experience. On the third hand... Hell, I hadn't even taken the case and was already counting on extra limbs just to keep track. And was he just going along with me or was there really an Oracle?

"Your Oracle can't tell you who did it?"

He shook his leonine head. "It doesn't work that way. The Oracle gets flashes of the future—not the full picture. Just fragments, usually of pivotal events. Apparently, Circe's murder didn't rate."

"But I did?"

Wow, that smile should be registered as a deadly weapon. "Apparently so."

Huh. Okay then. "What's your connection to Circe?"

"We were entering into a partnership. If her murder has anything to do with the business, I need to know."

"Very sentimental."

His laugh was a surprise, deep and even more intimate than his smile. It washed over me with a tingling heat, sending a hormone cocktail shooting through my veins. It took everything I had not to gasp.

My lids had started to lower when he stopped and speared my gaze with his own.

"It has been a very long time since anyone has taken me to task. I think we'll get along very well, you and I."

My body responded to that despite the warning klaxons blaring away in my brain. The urge to satisfy my curiosity warred with my need to get him the hell out of my office before any other needs became more urgent.

"Take it down a few notches or this conversation is over," I said, digging nails into my palm to try to redirect my focus.

Apollo eyed me, gaze too intense. Anger started thankfully to override my erotic impulses.

"Sorry," he said finally. "You took me aback and I let down my guard." He closed his eyes momentarily and something I couldn't put into words shifted, as if his presence dampened.

I sucked in a deep breath and took my time letting it out, trying to expel the tension along with it.

"That's what you're like *without* effort?" I asked, glad to hear that I sounded almost normal.

He shrugged. "It's a curse."

"I'm sure."

"No, really. I understand that it can be...overwhelming. I've lost—" He stopped there.

Either he was as good an actor as advertised or he really did know. Based on the old tales, I wouldn't have been the first to run from rather than into the fire.

"About that, why's an actor getting into the talent biz?" I asked, suddenly uncomfortable with the intimacy.

His eyes flashed, lighting an answering flash fire in me that could be either fear or excitement. "Don't be coy, Ms. Karacis. Ask the question that's really on your mind."

Whatever powers Apollo possessed, he certainly wasn't a mind reader if he thought I could narrow it down to just one question.

But in the end, maybe I could—if I could figure out a way to phrase it without sounding stupid.

"Are you—I was wondering about the origin of your name."

Apollo's, I don't know, *aura* dimmed further and it was as though a cloud had passed before the sun.

"Oh no, it is your limb. I will not test it for you. It will save time if you simply accept, and I do not like to dance around when we can get straight to...*business.*"

His eyes had a lock on mine, denying me the comfort of looking away.

"Fine. So you're a god," I said, going him one better and making it a statement. "Why acting then? Why lower yourself to reading someone else's lines? And why leave at the top of your game to manage other talent?"

He offered a feral smile. "Better. Yes, I am *that* Apollo or Hobal or Shamash or any number of gods in any number of cultures. Names do not have the power they're believed to possess. What you call someone is less important than the fact that you call him at all. As to how far we have fallen—that story, my fair lady, can fill volumes. Suffice it to say, as we turned from men to fight amongst ourselves, so they turned from us. Now, we must sing for our supper."

"But—"

He held up a hand to stop me. "By the time we realized that the tithes had dried to a trickle and the cupboards were bare, we were too late—other gods had taken root and we discovered, to our shame, that our powers had waned along with our worship. We had not the power to oust the usurpers. Ancient history."

My mind was reeling, a million thoughts vied for attention, chief among them that Yiayia would give her right arm to be in my place, meet *the* Apollo, ask and receive answers.

"I tell you this," he continued, "only to let you know what you're up against. We may no longer rule the earth, but we are far from powerless. This case will be dangerous, even for you."

Even for me—what was that supposed to mean?

"Why leave acting? I'd think the idolatry would be just like old times."

He answered with a wry grin. "I can only pass off my failure to age for so long. Sooner or later, I will have to start taking on," his lips curled, "*paternal* roles. I had thought that perhaps it was time for a sideline."

"You mean, besides the whole psychic gig?"

"Like I said, business is down."

"Okay, so you've done the prognostication thing and the acting, that still leaves a lot of time unaccounted for since your heyday. What've you and the others been doing all this time?" Yiayia might know, but she'd throttle me if she ever found out I'd had the chance to ask and didn't.

But Apollo was already shaking his head. "Need-to-know basis," he said, "and you don't—"

"Need to know. I've got it. Fine, enough about you. Let's talk about me—what do you mean dangerous to investigate *even for me?*"

He stared and I wondered if I'd finally managed to set him aback. "Don't you know?"

I stared back. "Let's say I'm in denial. Buy me a clue?"

He raked me up and down. "You've got to be kidding me. You're practically glowing with it."

"With what?" I asked, frustrated.

"Power."

I snorted. "Whatever. Okay, so let me get something straight—you've got this problem having to reinvent yourself because you don't age. Meanwhile, Circe's got to pull a Lady Bathory and practically bleed peasants to achieve the same result?"

His eyes widened. "I wondered about that. She's what? Second generation, I think, one of Helios' brats. The thing about Circe is—was—no one prolongs contact beyond the necessary. She's a shrewd businesswoman, but you'd check for keys, wallet and soul on the way out, if you know what I mean. So, I didn't ask and she didn't tell."

"I see. Very ostrich of you."

"Ostrich?" he asked, cocking his head to one side.

"Head in the sand. You know—it's not as if you fell down from Olympus yesterday."

The blinding smile was back. "I just like hearing you explain."

I rolled my eyes. "I know. I'm cute when I'm flustered. Look, save the charm for Jesus. He'll get a lot more out of it. I'll have him set you up with a contract and you can give him the retainer."

"Does this mean I'm dismissed?" he asked, radiating amusement.

Hell, the harder I tried to give him the "no go" sign, the bigger his smile.

"Not just yet. I want to run the killer's description past you—see if it rings any bells."

He shrugged. "You can try, though if we're dealing with one of the old ones, there's no guarantee he was wearing his true form."

"You assume it was a man."

Again he shrugged. "It is my understanding from the news reports—the police themselves told me very little—that the physical damage was extensive. While the female of the species might be deadlier than the male, it's been my experience that they're also more subtle and less likely to get their hands dirty doing the deed."

It was a sweeping generalization and, like most, riddled with exceptions, but not unreasonable.

"Ah, well, in this case anyway, I think you are correct, though I see no reason that a—" I choked on the word god, "—being that could shift form wouldn't choose to look like everyone else. This guy stood out—tall, scaly, green."

"I see your point. Still, scaly and green covers a lot of territory. Any of the water divinities would fit your description, though it probably puts Poseidon in the clear, since he's got a reputation of shifting for every piece of tail..."

"Thanks so much for your help," I said struggling not to roll my eyes. "One more thing before you go—I'll need access to Circe's files."

"Let me know when you'd like to view them and I'll set it up."

I nodded. No point wading in until I had more of an idea what I was looking for.

Apollo rose to leave, once again drawing my gaze to a completely inappropriate inventory of his attributes. I stepped back as he stepped forward, then realized how silly that was. There was an entire desk between us, and he probably meant only to shake my hand. Perfectly normal, like sealing the deal.

I forced myself to meet his eyes, already heartily tired of the amusement I knew I'd find, and raised a hand to shake. The jolt as he wrapped his long fingers around my hand caught me unaware, and for the first time in my life I almost understood the meaning of swoon. My knees felt a little weak as he turned the hand over and breathed across the knuckles before kissing them. Then he was gone. At least he'd had the decency to close the door behind him so that Jesus wouldn't find me in a puddle on my chair.

Chapter Four

"Windex, feh. What is this Windex joke everybody keeps making? Anybody with a brain knows Ouzo is the secret. Then if you're not better, who cares. Pain's gone."

—Helen Karakis, one third of the Karacrobats

"Detective Lau already offered me a cup of the paint stripper you guys call coffee, so I'm guessing she's got the role of bad cop for the day," I said by way of an icebreaker. Not that I didn't appreciate the strong silent type, especially when he came tall, dark and intense, but Armani's silences spoke volumes. Right now, we were on volume "A" for "Annoyed" that I'd delayed my visit to the station.

He arched one very effective brow.

"Might even be considered attempted murder if she made it herself," I babbled on.

"If McCarthy made it, I'd say you had a case. Worst Lau's coffee will do is strip your stomach lining."

"Assault then."

Armani inclined his head.

"*Okay*, I get it," I said, exasperated. "*Bad Tori, no cookie.* You can spank me later. For now, can we start over?"

"You mean pretend it's yesterday?"

"Yes, fine, pretend I followed you straight back to the station to make a statement. You know, it's not like I meant to fink out on you—" I stared at the pea-soup walls of the interview room while I contemplated just how much weakness I was willing to reveal to distract Armani from prying. "I've just never witnessed a homicide before. I needed time to process. You know that the more distance you get, the more detail you're able to remember."

"And the more time your brain has to fill in gaps with things not actually seen."

He had me there. Still— "I've had training. Besides, if I can't distinguish truth from fiction you're up shit's creek when you get me on the stand. So, I guess it's up to you. Do you trust me enough to look at mug shots now or am I just wasting your time and mine?" I challenged.

Armani glared me down, nostrils actually flaring, those wild, sexy brows lowered to shadow his eyes, darkening them to indigo.

I couldn't help it; I winked. He snorted.

"Dammit, woman, you've missed your calling. I think you could talk rings around half the lawyers in this town."

"Only half?"

"The other half work for Disney."

"Point taken. Tell me, you sweet-talk all your witnesses this way?"

"Lady, if that passes for sweet talk in your world, you're hanging with the wrong men."

"Occupational hazard," I answered with a shrug. "Whaddaya gonna do?"

He nearly had an answer for that, I could tell by his face as he bit it back. Armani's face was exquisitely expressive, especially for anyone trained to notice. And observation was invaluable to a successful carney, whose whole effect could be ruined by choosing the wrong volunteer—one who would flinch or try too hard to become part of the act or, worse, a debunker. Fortune-telling, by far my most successful attempt to fit into the circus, was really nothing more than good old Holmsian observation. Totally about the read, the show, giving the mark something to talk about later with friends. No one with an iota of sense really wanted to know the future. The big, life-altering events, the ones true psychics most often glimpsed, were generally cataclysmic and *not* fit for a day's entertainment.

Still, observing was a far cry from mind reading and there wasn't much I wouldn't give for the inside track on Armani's thoughts. I didn't think he'd trade them for the traditional penny, even inflated for the changing times. Of course, listening would probably have been a good start.

"—go over your statement before you run off again. So, why don't you look this over and see if there's anything we forgot or that you've thought of since yesterday while I go grab the mug books."

I sighed and settled in for a long sit in the ergonomically challenged chair. Before I was halfway through the statement, I'd shifted three times, finally kicking my shoes off, tucking one foot underneath me and settling one elbow on the table to support the arm holding my head. *Maybe I shouldn't have been so hasty turning my nose up at that coffee,* I thought as I stifled a yawn.

"Green around the gills," I muttered, reading from my own statement at the scene. "Did I really say that?"

Apparently, I had. And since Armani, as I knew from experience, had an eidetic memory, it had been duly noted. By the time Armani returned with the mug books, I was horrified by the facts and omissions, but most especially the many, many ways things could come back to bite me. Like if the police ever found the guy and wondered how I could miss the highly notable scales and webbing. Or if they never found the perp, as seemed more likely, and I was laughed out of the station house as a delusional freakazoid.

"Um," I started brilliantly, as Armani sat beside me. "Any other witnesses mention anything odd?"

He pushed his chair back from the table to get enough distance to really watch me. "Nooo," he answered slowly, "but I get the sense that one or two were holding back. Probably not ballsy enough to comment on any fishiness."

I froze, hand hovering above the mug book I'd been about to open. Armani knew something.

"Oh?" I asked, hardly trying for casual since my little freeze-frame had no doubt given me away. "So that's where you guys keep your courage—the balls. It's a wonder you're able to dredge it up fast enough in a crisis. See, us women, we're just infused throughout. So, what's fishy?"

"Think you're going to get away with the balls comment through redirection?"

I peered up at him through my lashes. "Not really. Just interested to see how you prioritize your response."

He growled, and I figured I'd pushed my luck about as far as I could go. Trying for my wings and halo, I flipped through a few pages of the book, studying each face as if I had some hope of finding the killer among them.

"They found piscine DNA mixed with human in the sample beneath Circe's nails," Armani said finally.

Based on his casual tone, which mimicked mine of earlier, I half expected to see him gazing nonchalantly down at his cuticles or whatever men did. I was not expecting to glance up directly into the supernova intensity of his gaze. He'd been studying me as he lobbed the information with a probing look that seemed capable of penetrating straight to my soul. No doubt I'd be squirming for an entirely different reason if I were guilty of some crime. As it was, it shot a tingle of awareness through me, starting round about my stomach and shooting all-point bulletins to the rest of my body. Oh yeah, it was getting hot in here. Surprisingly, Apollo hadn't completely shorted out my system. 'Course, it seemed to be on a hair trigger when it came to Armani.

"Really?" I asked, trying to ignore the sudden hot flash. "Contaminated sample?"

He looked at me like he knew I knew better—which, of course, I did. Most people, unless it was in their interest to mislead, didn't like to let a falsehood stand, mostly because it gave them a chance to one-up someone else. With Armani I wasn't trying to catch him out, since he had exponentially more experience than me at interrogation; I just wanted to give him an excuse to keep talking.

Instead, he shook his head. "Your turn. I need to know—are you working this case or did your involvement end with Circe's death?"

I debated the merits of cooperation.

"We're working on a subpoena for all records relating to Ms. Holland, but you can save us a bit of time," he added.

That decided me. Nothing to lose, information to gain.

"Sorry. You're not getting rid of me that easily. I've got a client, as of this a.m.," I answered.

"The one with the proposal?"

"No, someone new."

"You've got to give me more than that. Name? Leads?"

I took in a deep breath and let it out slowly to give myself time to think. I *really* didn't want to hear Armani's surprise that Apollo Demas would come slumming to me. Plus, passing on the kind of leads I had would probably get me an express trip to a rubber room.

"Apollo Demas," I answered finally. "And before you ask, someone told him I was already investigating."

"Great, so we may have a leak in the department."

I shrugged. "Could have been anyone at the salon yesterday. Place like that caters to the crème de la crème. Likely someone who knows someone overheard my name and figured they could curry favor by passing it along." *That or the Delphic Oracle,* I thought. "I wouldn't sweat it. Your turn."

"Leads?"

"No way, all you've given me so far is piscine DNA."

I remained stubbornly silent thereafter and finally he grunted, guy-speak for *whatever.* "Well, if you hadn't mentioned the perp's unusual appearance, we'd just figure he worked at a fish market or something, go from there. As it is, we think he may be some kind of fetishist."

"Gee, thanks for taking me there," I said, wrinkling my nose. "Who came up with that theory?"

He gave me the stink-eye. "Beats Lau's theory that you're self-medicating a mental illness."

Hard to argue with that when no doubt I'd think the same if positions were reversed. Armani had given me a whole lot of credit to take my observations, far out as they were, under consideration. I was touched. In the head, according to Lau.

Our eyes met and we had a brief moment of real connection, where I was startled enough to drop the in-your-faceness I normally used as a shield and Armani, seeing it drop, was startled enough to spot the person behind the banter. I had the strange urge to tell him everything—the crazy contract clause, "gods" walking the earth, dogs and cats living together. Okay, I'd borrowed that last one. Armani hit me that way. But I still only half believed it all myself. Besides, even family would betray you in the end, so there was no chance I'd be pouring out my heart to a virtual stranger any time soon.

"Thanks," I said without a trace of irony. It wasn't what I'd meant to say.

Armani nodded, the break in eye contact giving me the chance to recover from my temporary insanity.

I waved a hand at the mug books, back to business. "Well, I don't see a single aqua-boy in the batch. Guess I'd better get back to work and drum up some leads to earn my keep."

I was out of my chair and halfway to the door before Armani stopped me, an overheated hand on my arm transmitting warmth right through my sleeve. I didn't turn, not sure I wanted to look him in the eye with my hormones getting jiggy.

"Word of warning—brass is all over this like ugly on an ape. Sharing information could take you a long way, but if you withhold evidence, if you get in the way...it won't be pretty."

"That a threat?" I asked, knowing it wasn't. It was just easier to get my back up than acknowledge his concern.

"*Tori*," he said, shocking the hell out of me and making me look at him, "I'm serious. You become persona non grata and it will be worth any cop's badge to so much as talk to you."

"Don't tell me you'd miss me," I teased.

"You've been useful a time or two," he answered, but there was a glint in his eye.

It was ridiculous, really, the way any indication of interest from Armani gave me a little thrill. You'd think my gazillion failed relationships would have taught me better. No one withstood the spotlight of my attention for long. Not even my family had come through unscathed. Or maybe it was me who'd been scathed, since I'd only been trying to save my brother from himself, not open Pandora's box. But even in the circus I'd been a freak among freaks.

It would almost be a blessing to lose my lifeline to Armani— that way I couldn't be tempted to set myself up for rejection. *Yeah*, my mental mini-me scoffed, *too bad you're too damned proud to throw the game.*

Chapter Five

"Some family trees bear fruit, some nuts. Take a wild guess about ours."

—*Kostas Karacus, youngest third of the Karacrobats to his first non-folk girlfriend, who lasted all of a week*

If I was going to acknowledge Circe's and Apollo's existence on any level—and, despite myself, it seemed I already had—it was time to pull out the big guns. I found myself a nice, casual sidewalk café, chose a shady trellis table off to the side, ordered an iced latte and a scone from a hovering waiter and whipped out my cell phone.

I suppose it was a testament to my lack of a social life that Yiayia was number one on my speed dial. I couldn't remember where the circus was supposed to be this week, but it hardly mattered what time zone they were in. If there were two things Yiayia rarely did, they were sleep and shave. Shave because, well, it's pretty much antithetical to the whole bearded-lady gig. The beard? One of the more blatant demonstrations of the family's gorgon blood I'd managed to ignore all these years.

According to "myth", the gorgons not only had beards, they had serpents for hair and tusks as well. By all accounts a lovely bunch. Thankfully, tusks seemed to be recessive. Not a single freak growth in living memory—discounting my cousin Tina's really aggressive overbite.

The whole insomniac thing was a little more complicated and a lot more lucrative. It stemmed from the fact that Yiayia was constitutionally unable to transition to sleep mode. It goes like this:

1. Yiayia's brain had developed without a shut-off valve.

2. She's paranoid about medication—not to mention inorganic food, vaccinations and anything with too many legs, but those are another matter—and refuses to take sleeping pills.

3. She has a particular obsession with the lives, past and present, of the Greco-Roman pantheon.

4. She is not exactly in danger of becoming independently wealthy or even garnering a decent pension plan working for the circus, and...

5. Ever since Pappous passed away—the strong man with the weak heart—Yiayia had needed a hobby.

She'd managed to turn her obsession and all that dead time into a fiscally rewarding, Internet-based sideline business called *Mythography*. Oh, she wasn't silly enough to give away the current whereabouts of the various gods and goddesses. No one wanted to get on the wrong side of, say, the god of war, and Hera's hissy fits were legendary. But everyone liked to be related to someone famous. What Yiayia did was family trees and histories leading back in some way to a Greco-Roman god, goddess or hero. The way they all went nuts with their begetting, it wasn't too tough to do. If a family had any Mediterranean blood whatsoever, chances were she could find an "illustrious" forbearer. There was no telling how seriously the clients took the whole thing. I'd always thought it a load of crap, but Yiayia treated it as a mission.

Which was a really long way of saying that my grandmother pretty much had the goods on everybody. If I was looking for old blood, Yiayia was my one-stop shopping center for a suspect list with current whereabouts. Plus, she was one of the few members of the family still speaking to me.

She answered on the first ring. "Sweetie, honey, bubbelah— you don't call, you don't write."

I rolled my eyes. "Yiayia, I keep telling you, nobody really talks like that out here. And we spoke last week."

She spat out an obscenity in Greek that roughly translated to "bow-legged sheep lover". "*That* was before the great witchy-woman crashed and burned. And *you*, my own flesh and blood, who I nursed through scrapes, stitches and broken hearts, didn't even call to give your dear Yiayia the scoop."

Uh oh, she was talking about herself in the third person. I was in for it. "I'm calling now," I pointed out.

"Yes? Out of the goodness of your heart and to give me all of the dirt?" she asked facetiously.

"Sounds like someone already gave you the dirt. I swear, you've got a better network of informants than I do." Not that *that* was saying much.

"It is true," she announced smugly. "So, you called to pump me for information then? It will cost you. When do you come visit?"

"When pigs fly," I muttered.

"What is this?"

"As soon as Lenny Rialto retires," I amended.

"*Agape*, that is water under the bridge."

"So he no longer spits when he hears my name?"

"Well—"

"I rest my case."

"You will come when we are on hiatus. Or I will come to you," she threatened.

And that was only the upfront fee. The hidden cost was that I had to go through my story three times—until Yiayia could repeat it virtually verbatim—before the wily old bat would dish her own dirt. My cell phone was down to the last bar before I finally got the skinny on all area ancients. Who knew that Aphrodite had become the new Mayflower Madam or that Hephaestus now went by the name of Hiero Cholas, the reigning wunderkind of ILM?

Once Yiayia finally worked her way around to the fish-folk rumored to be in the area, I got more than I bargained for. I was hoping for something along the lines of Poseidon spotted completely knackered in some dive on Venice Beach ranting about how Circe'd done him wrong. Instead, I got an earful. It turned out a whole pod of oceanids and nereids had recently been spotted in the area, apparently having come to see the filming of a new mermaid movie. I knew vaguely of the film because Christie had been bummed that the timing of her Clairol commercial conflicted with the film's casting call.

So, I had a plethora of suspects with no current whereabouts, since they'd dispersed when the filming moved on from the waterfront. The land-based gods, Yiayia informed me, were so much easier to track, but until someone tagged the oceanids... I wasn't completely sure she was joking.

By the time we wound down, my latte was nothing but ice, my scone was mere crumbs, and the waiter, who must have heard enough to brand me a loon, was giving me sidelong glances.

"Okay," I said, playing to my audience, "I'll input those changes and have the revised script to you next week."

Yiayia had a good laugh at my expense. "Maybe *I* should write a screenplay. Make it very juicy and let all the gods and godlings pay me to suppress it. I might finally have enough to retire."

"Yeah, or you might find yourself turned into a shrubbery. Anyway, in order to blackmail someone, they have to have shame. Guessing that's not real big with this bunch."

Her sigh came through loud and clear. "Perhaps not then."

"Yiayia, this contact of yours—who is it? Anyone that clued in might prove a valuable contact on this case."

I didn't expect the loaded silence that greeted me.

"I can't tell you."

"What? Who're you talking to—Deep Throat?"

"Don't get smart with me, missy. I'll ask him myself if he knows anything, but you're on their radar now. If he's discovered talking to you, well, I don't think the others would be any too happy. I can't ask him to expose himself. He wouldn't even be speaking with me if not—"

I didn't know whether to be annoyed or intrigued. "If not what?"

"If not for our history," she said, as if I'd dragged it out of her. "There, you happy? I said it."

Yiayia had a history? She couldn't mean... No, no, I just had a dirty mind. Dealing with the gods would do that to a person. She'd known Grandpa since she was a teenager. *Didn't mean she'd never had any wild oats to sow*, my troublesome inner voice chimed in. *Eww!* I responded, hopefully not out loud.

"Okay, let me get this straight. Your contact is one of them—with a capital 'T'. This sinister *They* to which group Apollo, who's not only spoken to but hired me, belongs would get medieval on this guy's ass if he talks to me? Have you started back on your soap operas? Been dipping your beak into Pappous's bourbon stash? I don't understand all the secrecy. You'd think They'd make some sort of flashy announcement, throw a parade complete with banners: 'We're here, steer clear, turn over all your beer'."

"*Anipsi*," she barked. "Show some respect. Anyway, I'm not so sure nothing is afoot, which is why my, um, friend has to be careful."

Hmm, *very* interesting.

I sighed heavily. "Fine, have it your way. Just promise me that your guy is not green and scaly."

"He's not," she answered stiffly.

"Would you ask him for any scuttlebutt involving the fishfolk who had a beef with Circe?"

"Yes, if you agree not to try to hunt him down. I know how you are." I winced. "But now, my public awaits. We are in New York through Monday, but call me any time you have gossip. The next time I have to hear about you on the news, I will put on you the Spyropoulous hex."

I snorted. It was a good trick for psyching people out over cards, but somehow, I didn't think I had much to fear. "Yes, Yiayia," I said anyway. "I will call."

We rang off and I found that not only had my check arrived, but my waiter's card had come with. No doubt he hoped to be remembered when it came time to cast my fictitious script.

As I stared down at the card, inspiration struck. I had my very own Hollywood reference library on salary.

I flipped open my phone again as I reached for my wallet, then halted the latter impulse. If I wanted to foster the idea that I was a wheeler and dealer, I'd need to exude a sense of entitlement, not comfort the waitstaff that *yes*, I really did intend to move on someday and leave my table to someone willing to shell out for more than a scone and a latte. Certainly, the image would do well for me service-wise if I dropped by in the future, which, given the proximity to the cop show, seemed likely.

Jesus picked up on the second ring—always—said it gave the impression of too little to do to pick up on the first and too much to wait until the third.

"Good morning, Karacis Investigations," he said pleasantly.

"Hey, Jesus. I need your expertise. Would you get on the 'net and look up everything you can about the mermaid flick that's been filming out at Venice Beach? Cross-reference the cast list against Circe Holland's name. See what you can come up with."

"Oh hey," he responded, dropping the energized voice for his regular ennui. It just wasn't worth the effort for little old me. "You mean *investigate*."

I didn't need the Sight to figure out where he was headed—big client, money influx—Jesus was thinking raise. Ever the realist, I wasn't ready to count my chickens before they were fully grown.

"I mean *assist* in an investigation, yes."

He gave me a raspberry. "Spoilsport."

"Diva," I countered.

"That's aspiring diva to you. Speaking of which, I'll be out Friday; I have an audition." He followed up with a dramatic sigh. "I'll have everything on your desk when you return. You *are* coming back, right? You haven't run off with your studmuffin? You still have time for us little people?"

"And you are?" I asked.

He very properly hung up on me.

My waiter's eyes glowed as I pocketed his card and placed my money in the leatherette bill folder. He thanked me without even looking inside. I envied him the optimism of youth.

Chapter Six

"Living is just what we do to entertain and sustain ourselves until death. So, latte anyone?"

—Jesus

Jesus fairly leapt out of his chair the second he saw the whites of my eyes.

"Chica, you will not believe what I have found!" He paused dramatically for an appropriate expression of interest.

"Well, don't keep me in suspense," I obliged. I even sat in the reception chair beside his desk rather than make him follow me into my office to report.

"You will not believe the half of it. I mean, I'd heard the production was *cursed*, but I had no idea..."

"Jesus, any chance of you actually telling *me* what you learned any time today?"

He sniffed, but was too about-to-burst to withhold data as punishment. "Fine, the highlights. You know about Sierra Talbot's death, yes?"

"Um—"

He clicked his tongue in disgust. "She died in her bathtub three-quarters of the way through filming. No apparent cause of death. They'll have to CGI the rest of her scenes."

Oh, *that* Sierra Talbot. "Go on."

"Okay, so that's on top of walk-outs, damaged equipment. No big, right? Happens all the time. But here's the thing, some of the actors and even the crew claimed they saw strange things swimming around in the water—like, *mermen.* That's what the walk-outs were about—people too damned freaked to go near that water. And you *know* how freaked that's got to be. I mean, hello, beaches are pretty much our *raison d'etre.* Besides, water's going to swallow us sometime."

I rolled my eyes. "Well, aren't you just Mr. Shiny Happypants."

Jesus gave me an answering eye-roll. "*Whatever.* I'm out. News, gossip, etcetera is on your desk."

He snapped his cuffs smartly into place and used the reflection off his computer screen for a last-minute touch-up of the hair before taking off.

"Jesus, you're a prince," I called after him.

He acknowledged me with an airy over-the-shoulder wave.

I sighed and turned to the paperwork awaiting me in my office. With Jesus gone, it was too damned quiet. I never could think in silence. Before turning to the papers Jesus had stacked neatly in my inbox, I hit a key on my computer to wake it up and reached for my CD case. *Smash Mouth* called to me, but they always made me want to *move.* Good for cleaning or pacing, bad for reading. *Offspring,* I decided instead, especially since there was no one around to hear if I unconsciously hummed along. Jesus had threatened a strike the first time he'd heard me; asked if there was a level beyond tone deaf— seventh level of hell, maybe.

Music playing, I kicked off my boots, propped my feet up on the desk and focused on the printouts. Two things stood out. One, there'd been a lot of noise about the mysterious nature of Sierra Talbot's death at first, but no post-autopsy follow-up in the press. Maybe the reality was too much of a letdown after the buildup. Or maybe the police were keeping mum. If Sierra had been one of Circe's clients and had her life force drained, cause of death might well have eluded the ME. And two, special effects were being done by none other than ILM. Hiero Cholas had been mentioned by name.

I wondered if Armani already knew about a link between Circe and the little mermaid and if that was a contributing factor to his consideration of the fetish angle. If I wanted to learn more about the official file on Sierra's death, I was going to have to turn up something to trade. Hiero seemed as good a place to start as any. The trick was getting to him.

I could think of only one way. I tried to tell myself that calling Apollo was perfectly natural. He was my client; I needed a connection he could provide to help the investigation. Anyway, the number he'd left probably only got me as far as his personal assistant. Even so, my heart started to beat faster. It felt too much like asking a favor—and favors generally came with strings.

Still, I'd have to cave sometime if I wanted a look at Circe's files, which I did now more than ever. 'Course, even if it turned out that Circe had repped Sierra and planted the nasty little clause in her contract, I couldn't see any immediate connection to the fish folk. As trails went, it ranked right up there with Hansel and Gretel's breadcrumbs.

I picked Apollo's card off the edge of the desk where he'd left it and studied the number, memorizing for later reference, and froze as I found myself actually stroking the card with my thumb. Weird, weird, weird. Not to mention creepy. Which begged the question, could I really blame the strange obsession on Apollo's godly mojo when he wasn't even in the room? If not, what did that leave? I refused to consider myself a shoo-in for the starring role in Fatal Attraction II, though I was certainly in the right place for it.

Moving on, I shook off the self-analysis. Probably, it was just the superior paper quality making me all touchy-feely. I had a job to do and failing to make the call would only be wussing out.

I dialed the office phone, hoping with each ring to get bumped to voice mail, which was just stupid, since I'd get a lot further a lot faster if we connected. Besides which, if Apollo called back, he'd get me on *his* timing when I wouldn't be steeled against the sound of his voice.

For a wonder, the universe passed up an opportunity to thumb its nose in my general direction and a prerecorded voice popped on to ask me to leave a message. I did so—coherently even.

I chewed my lip as I thought about other avenues for research. It was too soon to hear anything back from Yiayia, considering she was on stage and all. I thought briefly about trying to hack into her phone records to track down her contact, but I was strictly amateur. I could manage to infiltrate the average person's home computer, but the phone company was another matter and not worth the jail time. Besides, I'd promised. Sort of.

Luckily, my phone rang before I could contemplate any further felonies.

"Karacis Investigations," I answered in my receptionist voice.

"Hello. Tori Karacis please."

My eyes nearly rolled up into my head. Hearing my name in that deep, resonant, vaguely accented voice was enough to give me palpitations.

"Speaking," I answered, determined not to show the effects.

"Ah, I thought that it might be. You rang. Have you discovered something already?"

The question was inevitable, and I was prepared. I fed him enough to satisfy him about the police investigation and my own leads with the standard disclaimer that it was early yet and that other avenues of inquiry were certain to materialize, yada, yada, yada.

"I called because I need three things from you. First, an appointment to review Circe's records—"

"Fine," he cut in and rattled off a number. "That will get you to Circe's administrative assistant. I'll tell her to expect you."

"Okay then. Next I need an introduction to Hiero Cholas."

"Hiero—why?"

"Routine. He's got ties to the nereids, having been raised by one if the myths have it right, and to the mermaid film via ILM. If either have any connection to Circe's death, he's a likely source of information."

"I'm not—" he paused, and I could almost hear him changing gears. I wondered what he'd been about to say and why he'd stopped. "I'll see what I can do. Third?"

"I'd like to talk with one of the oceanids or nereids myself if you can arrange it."

"Alas," —*Alas?*— "that I can't do."

"Why?" I asked when he failed to elaborate.

"It's—delicate. Let's just say that an introduction from me, even if I knew how to contact them right now, would do you more harm than good."

Translation, I guessed, amounted to *yet another failed affair where the pursuee ended up transmogrified, pregnant or stranded.*

A tart comment tickled the tip of my tongue, but I bit it back. Kicking a god when he was down, however much he might deserve it, didn't seem the wisest course.

"I'll find my own path then. Thanks for your help."

"It is nothing. Please, call me any time. And I mean that."

His voice had lowered to phone-sex level on that last, and I was suddenly shivery in some very intimate places. I had to swallow to lubricate my dry throat before I could respond. By the time I did, it was too late. Apollo had disconnected, leaving my body humming completely out of sync with the dial tone.

I deliberately forced my mind back along more fruitful pathways. Yiayia couldn't be the only mortal who'd twigged to the whole "immortals walking the earth" concept. Maybe I could find someone on the web who was less discrete about giving away current info. I'd have to wade through a lot of crap probably, but if something big was churning up the rumor mill, as Yiayia had implied, there was a good chance I'd find something. The Internet was like one gigantic small town. The question was what in the world did I type in to find a needle in a haystack? I couldn't very well just enter "trouble in godland" and expect all my problems to be solved.

Or maybe I could.

My fingers flew over the keys. No, no, I couldn't. I tried about a dozen more searches in both English and Greek and followed hoards of completely useless links before finally lighting on a likely site.

I browsed for a while, learning fun facts like that Zeus was currently performing at Caesar's Palace in Vegas as Zeus Stormbringer, his act a "dazzling pyrotechnic extravaganza". So heartwarming to see the gods using their powers for good.

Then there were silly sections like the "Find Your Inner God(des)" personality quiz and the "Gotta Getta God" word search, but my favorite, the section I was searching for, was the rap sheet, a gossip-rag-styled list of hints, allegations and things left unsaid.

It was intriguing to speculate on who'd starred in a series of porn films in the early '70s under the names Ray Long and Venus Wells, not that the latter took a great deal of imagination. Venus—Aphrodite—too easy. And Ray, hmm, a sun god maybe, like—no, it couldn't be. A grin spread across my face. Our very own Apollo? Well, hey, he wouldn't be the first to transition from, ahem, *adult film* into mainstream theatre. Tracy Lords was probably the best known, but there were plenty of never-squelched rumors about Sly Stalone and Marilyn Monroe. I tried really hard not to linger too long on any images that wanted to take my mind off legitimate research.

Lords knew how much time I'd wasted before finding a single hint of useful information halfway down the rap sheet: "Rumor has it that some pretty elemental forces are coming together to stage a comeback. So, what I'm wondering is, are we all about to be thrown together into one big melting pot, complete with scalding, or are we in for the mother of all clambakes? Only time will tell."

Even as rumblings went, it was pretty sketchy. I tried to puzzle it out. Was the rumormonger trying to be cutesy or was there a method to his madness? The former would be no help at all, so I focused on the latter. Elemental forces. Okay: earth, air, fire, water. Melting pot—water to fill it, fire to heat it, earth for the pot? Or maybe the people within represented clay or salt of the earth. Clambake—again maybe water from which the seafood came with fire for baking. Even if I was on the right track, I couldn't see how that put me very far ahead. The list of water divinities stretched as long as my arm, from the great Oceanus through Poseidon down to the lowliest nereid. And fire? There was Apollo, of course; Circe's own sire, Helios; Hephaestus of the forge; even Zeus with his firebolts...

I could think of only one kind of comeback and it involved worship, tribute and debasement for us mortal saps. At least I could probably rule out Apollo. If he were staging a coup I couldn't see the sense of hiring me to poke around. Unless—unless Circe's death put a hitch in his plans. But then why choose me if he figured I'd be too dense to shed light on his own closeted skeletons? On the other hand, what harm could little ol' me do? It wasn't as if I could make the midnight ride waving my lantern and yelling, "The Olympians are coming!"

I was getting ahead of myself. I didn't even know that Apollo was involved or that the rumors were true. Even if they were, these gods had been quiescent for thousands of years. Who was to say that they held the power to change things now? Wouldn't they have risen up years ago if that was the case? It was probable that even gods had delusions of grandeur.

Somehow, my logic didn't entirely put me at ease. As Mel Brooks once wrote, "No one expects the Spanish Inquisition." In serious deconstructionist mode, I took that to mean that the reason terrible things happen is that moral, rational people just couldn't grasp the enormity of the horror in time to stop the juggernaut. Plus, the bad guys cheat.

Chapter Seven

"Tori fears to go where angels tread, but doesn't seem to mind digging in the dirt and turning up grubs. She must get that from your side of the family."

—Gus Karacis, second third of the Karacrobats

It was hard to think of Hiero Cholas, a.k.a. Hephaestus, a.k.a. Vulcan, as otherly abled or physically challenged or whichever moniker was currently in vogue. He had swoon-worthy shoulders that glistened with sweat where they were exposed by his Atlas Gym T-shirt, as if he really had just come from the forge rather than an airy loft, his *pied a terre* in L.A. He did walk a bit stiffly, though not for very long before he seated himself behind a drafting table covered end to end with disassembled electronics, some still twitching like remote-control cars when someone in the vicinity was playing on their frequency.

It was his face more than anything that made you think of the lameness that had gotten him cast out of Olympus by his own mother, Hera, simply for being imperfect. Not that there was anything wrong with the face, especially if you liked the brooding Heathcliff-type—it had fine, pale, tequila-colored eyes, strong squared-off lines, a powerful mouth. The problem was that Hiero looked like he was just waiting, daring you even, to mention his legs, at which point he would pounce like a wounded tiger. I felt that I could easily forget there was any vulnerability at all if only he'd let me. There was so much else to notice. But I didn't get the impression he gave anyone that chance. Being cast out at birth probably had that effect on a person.

The apartment was nearly as fascinating as the man, crawling as it was with movie monsters and disembodied parts. Hanging over the drafting table was a vampire bat with bloodied jaws, wings fully extended as if to launch another attack. Leering down from a bookshelf was a huge toxic-waste-green insect with sinister red eyes I recognized from the direct-to-video cover of *Mantis II*. A creature from *Death Strike*, which looked like someone had turned a manta ray inside out, was mounted on the adjoining wall.

"You like it?" Hiero asked, following my gaze. "The exoskeleton glows in the dark. Not the cheesy black-light effect, but luminous like a deep-water fish."

"Neat," I answered dutifully. "Your work?"

"Early stuff," he admitted. "That's why it's tucked away here. Sentimental value, but not my best work." The more relaxed look of memory lane vanished in an instant as he turned from his creations to me. And *wow* was that focus intense, even hostile. "You're not here to talk about my design work. Apollo says you want to discuss the old ones. For him you have five minutes."

I met his glare, thinking of how I'd like to deliver Hera a good smack-down for setting her son against the world right from the get-go. Of course, he'd had centuries to *get over it already.*

"Yes, I'd like to ask you about Circe and the filming of *Making Waves.*"

"What do you want to know?" Something leapt forward on the table and Hiero reached for it.

"What do you think is most relevant for me to know?"

He shook his head, not even sparing me a glance now from the gadgetry he'd begun to tinker with.

"I don't have time for a fishing expedition. Ask what you want and be done with it."

"Funny you should mention fishing. It seems that Circe was killed by one of the water divinities. Her attacker was green-scaled and webbed but walked like a man. Any idea who he might have been, who had a reason to kill Circe?"

"Yeah, Apollo gave me the description. I can't figure it. Thing is, most of the water spirits aren't amphibious. Aside from Poseidon, they're either built for the water or no different than you and me—or at least you—with an affinity for the water. And Poseidon wouldn't need to get his hands dirty to get rid of a little nothing like Circe. He doesn't even much concern himself with the land-dwellers anymore."

"Any particular reason?"

Hiero spared a second to glower at me. "His business."

I smiled to show I wasn't intimidated. "There can't be any harm in a little speculation."

"Fine, I'd *speculate* that things like the Exxon Valdez, garbage barges, PCPs and other dumping haven't really endeared mankind. Go figure." With a shrug, he turned back to his project, an eerily life-like robotic arm, now flexing and relaxing at the twist of a screw.

"Fair enough. What about Circe?"

"What about her?" he echoed. "You list the first hundred people who come to mind and I'll give you the whys and wherefores."

"How about the top ten?"

He snorted. "Yeah, like I've got a ranking system. You got a Bulfinches Guide? Start there."

I struggled not to grind my teeth. "How about the filming of *Making Waves*? Anything happen there that might have set someone off?"

He looked up and speared my gaze. I felt like a fish flailing at the end of a hook. "Lady, do I seem like the social type? I create my effects back at the workshop. I only get out as required to set things up and then it's straight back home. Circe repped the talent, but she didn't play handler, so I'd guess she never even appeared on-site. I can't see the connection. If that's all you've got, I think Apollo's wasting his money."

Such a charmer. He went back to tinkering.

"Well, hey, thanks so much for all your cooperation. Could you at least pinpoint for me the locations of the shoot? I'd like to see if any of the oceanids or nereids are still around to interview."

His brows rose, though his eyes didn't. Grudgingly, he hefted his bulk out of his chair, walked stiff-legged to his single filing cabinet and yanked on a drawer that whined in protest. I didn't see any tabs, just a mess of papers—glossy, blueprint, velum—all with ragged edges and seemingly tucked in any which way. He flipped through them quickly, flying past two or three pages at a time, clearly uncaring whether he found what he was looking for or not. Finally, though, he stopped, pulled out a map of coastline and thrust it at me.

I had to rise to accept it.

"Do you need these back?"

"The masters are on file somewhere. No need for you to come back."

In other words, *Don't let the door hit you on the way out.*

But I'd never let a little thing like social graces get in the way of my curiosity.

"What kind of effects did you do for the film?"

I hadn't noticed before, but his brow ridge was *really* pronounced when he scowled.

"Functional mermaid tails, kelp hair, that kind of thing," he answered, beginning to crowd me toward the door.

"Did you notice any of the nereids or oceanids hanging around?"

"Sure, the sirens and I had a little tea party, dined on barnacle stew." He reached around behind me for the door. "If there's nothing else—" a push that was more of a shove and the door shut in my face.

Wow, the charm was simply staggering. Finally, a man I'd want to bring home to mother. For a cage match.

Early spring was probably my favorite time to visit Venice Beach. Fall and winter were too tarted up for my taste with all the overblown seasonal displays. Summer was gorgeous, of course, especially if you considered it a perk to be cheek by surgically altered jowl with the bronze and the beautiful. Thongs as far as the eye could see. Speedos on men who could almost pull off the look. In the whole history of the world, the part I'd been around for anyway, there'd been maybe three men who could make the bikini bathing suit work—Greg Louganis, Mark Spitz and...okay, two men. Don't get me wrong, I'm a huge fan of the natural male physique. It was more the weight machine bulging-in-odd-places look that gave me trouble. I much preferred the taut, streamlined, natural approach. You didn't see much of that in L.A. But I digress.

By early spring, all that was done. Venice Beach, L.A. and its environs were as close to normal as they ever got. *Real?* Well, that was a matter of perspective. Out here keeping it real was just an expression, no more comprehended than "right as rain" or "sick as a dog".

On this beautiful April day people and street performers—fire-eaters, roller-blading musicians and stand-up philosophers—milled around on the boardwalk a quarter mile away. Farther still rose the scenic Santa Monica Mountains. Lovers might stroll at sunrise or sunset. But for now, I had the beach all to myself. Just the way I liked it.

I didn't know what I expected to find, nigh on a month after filming wrapped, but it almost didn't matter. The sun was shining, as it did three-hundred-plus days of the year. The breeze was blowing. My slingbacks knocked against each other as I held them, allowing my toes to curl into the deliciously chill sand. Life was good.

Murder? It was the farthest thing from my mind.

That was the kind of effect the ocean had on me, when I could actually hear the crash of the waves over the roar of the people.

I wandered up and down what I estimated to be the right section of beach, futilely stooping to examine the occasional bit of detritus. If anything of the fish-folk had been left behind, the ocean had claimed it. Finally, I approached the water, which rode in to the beach on gentle four-foot waves, sadly underestimating the tides. As I jumped back from the shock of ice-cold water, I caught movement beyond where the waves began. That froze me. I swept the spot again, hoping to find what had caught my eye, but there was nothing. A figment of my imagination or light hitting the rippling water just so. *Maybe.* But my hindbrain, the part that processed without conscious effort, wouldn't accept that. *Something* had been there. Too cold for swimmers, too tame for surfers. Anyway, either of those would have surfaced again.

Damn, I was going out there. I sat my shoes down in the sand with my jacket folded atop to await my return and rolled up my pants legs as high as they would go to just above the knee. I wouldn't get far, but it would have to do.

The water had only gotten as high as my ankles when my teeth started chattering. I hugged my arms to my chest, as if that would help, and bulled on ahead. Another step, a breaking wave, and the water was up to my knees. Still nothing. My gaze panned the ocean, catching flecks of foam here and there beyond the waves, but nothing *off.* One or two more steps, and I'd be risking the wrath of my dry cleaner. Plus, I was starting to lose feeling in my toes.

What the hell, I thought. *I've come this far. If need be, Apollo can spring for a new suit. Call it a business expense.* I waded forward and something brushed my feet. The chill suddenly hit my heart. Then that something wrapped itself around my leg and yanked. Hard. A scream ripped from me as I went down, opening my mouth to the rush of water—gagging, choking, burning and freezing at the same time as it raced down the wrong pipe, seizing my lungs. I thrashed, but the *thing* had hold of my leg, was pulling me into deeper water. I was desperate for air. My heart pounded but couldn't seem to expand, as if gripped by a tightening fist.

That panicked me. I jackknifed, clawing at the hand holding me—webbed, I noted as the skin separated. It was a grotesque feeling, worse because it came with a spike of triumph. The grip released. I kicked it away, straining toward the surface—what I hoped was the surface.

72

A single gasp of air, then the creature had me again, this time in a bear hug around the waist. It practically climbed my back, its body weight pulling me down as it leveraged itself up. Oddly jointed arms circled my neck, cutting off any aid from that last aborted breath. *Last.* No, I wouldn't accept it.

I kicked backward with all my strength, but had no leverage and his legs quickly wrapped around mine to keep me still. Defenseless. *He* because whatever sick fuck was behind me was getting off on the whole thing. I could feel it. I fought the urge to tense and instead played limp as if the fight had gone out of me, hoping not to telegraph my next move. In the following instant, I flung my head back, bracing against his very body as I smashed his face.

I felt something give and the arms went loose, just long enough for me to twist, to try to bring my arms up between us. It brought me face-to-face with Circe's killer. No time to dwell on the insanity of what I was seeing as his coal-black eyes met mine—or maybe those were spots swimming before me. Deep, dark, depthless. Already I felt myself slipping away from lack of oxygen. I hoped to Hades the family legends were true and focused everything I had into freezing my attacker in place with the glare.

Nothing moved. *Nothing.* We were sinking before my sputtering brain realized that meant it had *worked.* No treading was keeping us afloat. He was frozen.

Galvanized, I shrugged out of his arms and kicked for all I was worth in the opposite direction—up! My arms felt like lead and my legs like they were encased in cement, but I kept moving.

The urge to open my mouth, to breathe, became nearly unbearable. Spots became my landscape. I wasn't going to make it.

It was as if the surface rushed to meet me as I poured the last of my strength into one final kick. I hit the air coughing up water and taking oxygen in great gulps.

All I wanted to do was lie there floating, recovering my strength and just breathing, but somewhere below me that thing waited. I didn't know how long the paralysis would last— still couldn't believe my whammy had worked at all.

It seemed the hardest thing I'd ever done to make myself *move*. My arms and legs were stiff with cold and refused to bend. It was as if I beat the water with sticks. Only fear propelled me. Every time I bobbed upward I focused on the beach, but it never seemed to be any closer. Finally, my movements slowed almost to nothing except for the shaking. Tremors racked my whole body now. Hypothermia—or something. Something I was supposed to remember. I nearly sank before I thought to turn onto my back. To float. Sun blind. Helpless.

Something grabbed for me—*again?* I thought—but I didn't have enough energy to fight or figure out why that should be disturbing.

The world had contracted to my palsied limbs and the unexpected warmth of the grip. Dimly I realized that I was moving again, then I lost the fight with consciousness.

Chapter Eight

"All things being equal, I prefer life over death, 'cause, you know, I never have thought of a suitable comeback for that."

—Tori Karacis

I awoke to a slight pressure on my chest and lips on mine—vaguely, um, mushy—with breath definitely garlic-tinged pushing its way into my mouth. My gag reflex kicked in and the pressure disappeared as I curled onto my side in a fetal position and coughed up a noxious cocktail of saltwater and bile. The heel of a hand bruised my back several times, presumably to encourage the purge. It certainly did that—each time my head would swim and the vertigo caused me to heave-ho.

I was about ready to take a whack at the hand's owner when I realized something terribly important: I was alive. Pain was just a side effect.

"Ulg—" I managed as the hand hit me again.

A moment of blissful silence was observed. Then I rolled over only to be captured by the rapt stare of my green-haired, barely post-pubescent rescuer. *Sure,* I thought, *it couldn't have been Orlando Bloom or Hugh Jackman. Oh no, it had to be a refugee from Green Day.* It wasn't a thought I was particularly proud of, but apparently my inner censor hadn't yet recovered her equilibrium.

"You okay?" he asked earnestly.

Since the poor boy was still dripping wet, I was guessing I owed him for more than a little mouth-to-mouth.

When I didn't answer immediately, he added, "Jill called 9-1-1."

It was the first I noticed that there were other people around as well. Enough to start our own beach volleyball game.

I groaned.

"I saw you go down out there," he continued. "I didn't think there were sharks here, but I guess I was wrong, huh?"

I tried to shake my head and it nearly split in two.

It felt like someone with a crowbar was trying to whack his way out of my skull.

Seconds later, we were joined by paramedics, who oh-so-helpfully pushed aside the kids and shined an overly bright light into my eyes. I only let them live because 1) I was too weak to move farther and 2) they brought blankets.

It was all fun and games 'til they pulled out the stretcher, the better to cart me off to the hospital, at which point I became an instant convert to Christian Scientology—or whatever it was that claimed medical care was *Evil*. 'Cause everyone knows that evil spelled backwards is live.

Everybody stared at me as if I had two heads and had maybe conked them both too hard out there on a reef. The burlier of the two medics looked like he was ready to haul me in anyway—for a psychiatric exam if nothing else—but his partner held him back with a "Dude, we can't do it."

He turned to me then. "But, lady, if you don't go with us, you gotta get someone to come out here for you. There's no way you're going home on your own steam. You can't drive."

Burly rolled his eyes. "I'll get the paperwork," he said, and stomped off up the beach toward the ambulance.

From the 'tude, I was guessing refusal of care came with a cover-your-buttload of paperwork. But that wasn't my problem. My problem was that on my shoestring budget I never had gotten around to frivolous things like health insurance. The paramedics alone would probably bankrupt me. The hospital was right out.

Paperwork meant questions I shuddered to consider answering. My throat ached like I'd swallowed prickly pears. I tried to think of something that would head them off at the pass.

"Wallet," I croaked to the surfer dude, shakily moving to pat my pocket.

When I left my purse behind, I generally folded essentials— driver's license, PI license, gun permit, some cash and cards— into a bifold case that slipped into my pocket. I hadn't planned on going for a swim. I wondered what had fared worse, my body or various IDs.

Surfer dude took pity on my slow-motion attempt to fish out my wallet and finally did the honors. He took an inordinant amount of time flipping through everything, even letting an "oh cool" slip out at the sight of my PI license and carry permit, before finally stopping at one card with a hand-scrawled cell phone number. Armani's. I groaned as he turned it toward me in question and took a swallow—*big mistake*—before nodding my head in answer.

Armani was going to make me pay for this, but I didn't see any other option. I was pretty sure that the cell phone on my hip and all the nice numbers in memory had not survived the dunking.

My eyes must have started to close because the next thing I knew, I was getting slapped in the face. "Stay with us," surfer boy commanded.

"So tired," I mumbled.

But surfer boy had an answer for that—a series of rapid-fire questions to correspond to those little blanks on the paperwork attached to his clipboard. I tried answering each in ten words or less, wondering if they'd believe my near-death experience had spurred me to a sudden vow of silence.

By the time Armani arrived, the few gawkers—no big drama like spurting blood or writhing in pain to hold them—had melted away, including my rescuer, who I realized to my shame I hadn't even thanked. I was almost looking forward to whatever riot act Armani was sure to read me if only because he wouldn't expect an answer—at least, not until he wound down. Dashing my hopes, he drifted in silent as the grave to loom over the shoulder of my inquisitor after talking to the other EMT. His lips were tightly compressed, though, and I could tell this was just the calm before the storm.

When the questioning finally died off, Armani reached down to help me up and through sheer force of will I managed to get my muscles working so that I wasn't completely dead weight. The romantic image of being clasped to Armani's chest while he heroically bore me off into the sunset fell apart completely with the reality that the scene would more likely involve staggering and cursing under his breath. Not to mention the whole damsel-in-distress thing had never worked for me anyway.

Girl power and all that aside, though, there was something about Armani clutching me tight, his strong arm heating my gooseflesh that was maybe just a little gratifying. Add to that the fact that he wasn't even complaining that I was getting him completely soaked in the process and I was about ready to take him home to mother, but that seemed a piss-poor way to repay him.

As soon as Armani had me settled into the car with the heat cranked to full, he turned my way and I thought *here it comes.*

"Christian Scientology?" he asked, a glint in his eye.

My shrug was barely detectable. "No insurance," I rasped back. "Had to say something."

He looked like he was struggling not to smile. "I think they call themselves Christian Scientists."

"I'll—" I winced as the pain temporarily overwhelmed me, "—remember that."

Armani studied me for a few beats before reaching for his seat belt, adjusting my mirrors and generally doing the guy pre-flight check.

"Sounds like you're in a lot of pain right now, so I'm not going to ask, but as soon as you get some aspirin and dry clothes, I want the full story, even if you have to sign it to me."

I nodded meekly, made mellow by the warmth. My eyes shut of their own volition and the next thing I knew, Armani and I were parked out front of my apartment building and he was trying to wake me by chafing my hands. His face was less than a breath away from mine until he noticed that my eyes had opened.

Once inside, I felt like an invalid as I sat at what would have been my kitchen table had I had such a room and directed Armani toward pain meds and glasses via hand gestures. I tried not to notice that my studio apartment was not exactly in company condition—the pull-out sofa I slept on was still in disheveled bed mode, my jammie T-shirt slung over the side, dishes I'd been hoping elves would clean piled in the sink. But it seemed that Armani was most concerned with the fact that I was about to exceed the doctor-recommended dose of the generic painkiller he brought me.

"Reformed Christian Scientist," I said, hoping to bring back the smile I'd seen earlier.

"Uh huh," he responded.

"Um," *yikes*—okay, no unnecessary thinking noises. I mimed my way to the pad and paper beside my telephone.

I really appreciate you picking me up, I scribbled. *Really. But—*

"But what?" Armani asked, his voice gone cold. Apparently, his cop skills extended to reading upside-down chicken scratch.

Frustrated, I put down the pen. Writing was going to be too damned slow.

"I need a bath," I croaked, hand to my throat as if it would make any difference. "Right now I feel like I'd pass out bending over to start the water. I'd never have called you to begin with if—" my voice gave out, which was probably a good thing, given that what had been coming out sounded all wrong in my head. I swallowed and tried again, softer. "Not that you were my last choice. Just—I need a girlfriend."

Armani looked at me like a suspect he intended to crack, as if every word spoken had some other meaning. Finally, he swiped a hand hard over his face.

"Look, you witnessed a murder, came face-to-face with the killer. We probably should have set some sort of watch on you right from the first. My fault. But—dammit, by the time you're through flirting and baiting, it's a wonder I remember my own damned name," he growled.

I was flummoxed. "So I *do* get to you."

He practically glared. "Yeah, like that's a freakin' newsflash. Why else do you do it?"

"Because I can't help myself," I answered.

Damn and double damn. I should have stuck with the pen.

My admission didn't seem to make him any happier. "Look, you're a witness in an ongoing investigation."

"Yeah."

"And a pain in my ass."

I was tired, I was soaked to the bone, but as much as I wanted that bath and my bed...

"So?" I challenged.

"*So*, we can't do this."

"*Do what?*" I asked, exasperated. "We're not doing anything—"

In the blink of an eye, Armani had risen from his chair, taken my face in his hands and shut me the hell up with a kiss. And not just any tentative little first kiss—a breath-stealing, heart-pounding, fade-to-black kind of showstopper. I found I wasn't nearly as exhausted as I'd thought. With minds of their own, my fingers buried themselves in his hair, reveling in the feel of the thick strands, kneading his scalp. My thoughts scattered as his tongue thrust inside my mouth and I gasped in reaction.

His hands slid from my face, down over my wet camisole, just brushing my breasts before settling on my hips. I was no longer cold—superheated was more like it—but wet was another matter.

Armani pushed himself away. Without looking at me, he muttered, "I'll start the water running and wait just outside the door so I can hear you if you fall." And he escaped into the only other room in my apartment, the bathroom.

My head fell to the table in frustration and sudden weakness. In the time it took him to get things ready, a series of unworthy thoughts flitted through my mind—pulling him in with me, faking a fall, flat-out asking him to wash my back. But I wasn't going to trick Armani into anything. He either wanted me or he didn't.

Still, I couldn't help a bit of teasing, allowing a breast to brush his arm as he escorted me to the bath.

"I may need help with these wet clothes," I said, damaged throat making it come out all husky.

He shot me a sidelong look. "At this point, I don't think the bath would do those clothes any harm."

"*Such* a gentleman," I answered with a roll of my eyes.

"I am a gentleman. That's why you're on your own with those clothes." Then he decided to turn my teasing back on me. "Besides, if I were to take them off, I'd need to taste you right—" the hand not supporting me rose to ever-so-gently slide over my throat until his thumb caressed the hollow, "—here."

My nipples practically stood at attention, pushing noticeably against my camisole. The look he gave me was hot enough to scorch and smug besides.

I had no comeback.

"Speechless? Hmm, I'll have to remember that."

Which sounded promising, like maybe he'd do it again sometime, regardless of his "me heap big by-the-book cop" speech of earlier.

I wanted to give him something to remember all right, but with my legs wiggling like limp spaghetti, now didn't seem the time. We made it into the bathroom without incident—or rather I did. The room was barely big enough for me by my lonesome. Even toweling off presented challenges. Once I was through the door, Armani closed it behind me, leaving a gap too thin even for a peep show.

As soon as he heard me settle into the water, the grilling began, evaporating my pleasant erotic buzz. Why had I been on the beach? Was I investigating a lead I'd failed to share with the police? What the hell had I been doing in that water? What in the blue blazes had happened out there? Okay, he really didn't talk like that, but the effect was the same. I told him everything, quietly, painfully, including that I'd planned to go from the beach right to the station to talk about a possible link to Sierra Talbot's death, but when it came to what had happened, I pleaded for a break.

My throat felt like someone had attacked it with sandpaper and ammonia, but more than that I needed to think. If I told him I'd been fighting with the killer, he'd demand to know why I hadn't told him sooner. He might even insist on some kind of protective custody. If I didn't fess up, I'd have to invent a plausible explanation for my condition and my brain didn't seem to have thawed out just yet.

Generally, I'd found the truth, or a good portion thereof, would garner a lot less trouble than fabrication in the long run. In this case, though, with the truth so much stranger than fiction...

Getting out of the tub was like a really bad sitcom sketch—in a late-night slot due to the nudity and language. I got myself nearly upright before the strength in my legs gave up the ghost and they went straight out from under me. I bit down on a yelp to keep Armani from running to my rescue and grabbed frantically for the towel bar, which held for like a microsecond before coming half out of the wall and almost taking me down with it. I brought one knee up to catch my weight on the edge of the tub, but I was clumsy. Kneecap impacted with porcelain and exploded in pain.

Armani burst through the door at the commotion and grabbed me before the other half of the towel rack could give way. I clutched at him gratefully, as humiliating as it was, because the alternative was to go down in a soggy naked heap.

"You okay?" he asked, looking into my eyes and nowhere else.

My face had to match my burgundy towels, now spilling onto the floor, trailing in the puddle I'd created. "Sorry, I just, kinda, lost it for a second there."

"No problem. Want me to carry you?"

I think I made a sound something like *urk*. "No, but if you could get me—" my hand went involuntarily to my throat as it flared in pain, "—a robe."

I waved vaguely toward the peg at the back of the door. Armani eased me down onto the edge of the tub before slowly releasing me, watching all the while to be sure I wouldn't topple over in his absence.

As soon as he tossed the robe to me, I slid it carefully on, relieved to have even that much covering. The red silk wrap with black Chinese dragons climbing either side only came to mid-thigh, but it was enough. Unfortunately, I couldn't seem to make my shaking hands work enough to cinch it.

"Why don't I help you with that?"

Eyes averted to a cartoonish degree, Armani grabbed both ends of the belt and tied it into a hasty knot. Apparently, the sight of my naked body was just too horrible to face. *Or he's being a gentleman just like he said earlier,* my inner Pollyanna piped up. *Yeah,* my inner cynic retorted, *like any man with a pulse would willingly pass up a view of a woman in the buff.* It shouldn't have hurt so much. I was used to rejection, albeit a little farther down the road.

Okay, so my inner cynic had rebooted. Time to see if I could get my inner wench back online.

"I know how much that performance must have impressed you," I breathed, "but you think you can help me to my bed without losing all control?"

"I'll try to contain myself," he answered wryly.

He draped one of my arms around his shoulder and helped me creak to my feet and hobble to the edge of my bed.

"Turn around," I ordered.

Armani rolled his eyes. "It's not like I'm going to attack you or anything," he said, turning his back.

"Yeah, I got that loud and clear," I snapped. Great, a multiple personality free-for-all going on in my head and my inner censor was a no-show.

Unable to face Armani, I reached into the bedside table and snapped out a pair of panties to go under the oversized T-shirt I slept in.

He whirled me around by the shoulder, stunning the bejeebers out of me. "Dammit, what is your *problem*? Do you want me to attack you?"

I sneered at him, the best defense being a good offense. "Heavens no. Wouldn't want you to do anything distasteful."

"Freakin' women and their damn push-me-pull-you routine—"

"First of all," I barked, warming to the fight, "I don't see any other women here, so if you're going to insult me, at least treat me as an individual. Second, *you're* the one with the whole catch me, kiss me, grill me, ignore me shtick."

Armani's face was red verging on purple. "So your defense is that we're both screwed up."

"I didn't realize I needed a defense, *Detective*."

He threw his hands up in the air. "Fine. This was a lousy idea anyway."

"So you've said. Well, don't let the door hit you on the way out."

Armani stomped off, steam practically streaming out of his ears.

My throat ached. My heart—no, my pride—stung. You'd have thought that would be enough to keep me awake. You'd be wrong.

I went facedown on the mattress, exhaustion having its wicked way with me, and stayed that way. Before unconsciousness rose up to meet me, it flitted through my head that the argument had successfully quashed any further questioning about the events of the day.

Chapter Nine

"Freakin' gods, think they own everything."

—*Uncle Niko, just before getting fried in a freak electrical* storm

A blast of music shocked me awake hours later, kicking my heart straight into high gear. George Thorogood and the Delaware Destroyers had possessed my laptop.

Not that I realized that's what it was at first. Oh, no, not the way today was going. No, first I had to destroy my clock radio, thinking it was my freakin' alarm. It wasn't until that failed to stop the window-rattling rendition of "Who Do You Love?" that I blearily looked around for the source and discovered a shimmering image whirling ever larger on the black screen of my laptop, which should have been both closed and off.

Great, I thought, none too clearly, now I've got a computer virus on top of the rest of today's weirdness. I stumbled out of bed and over to my desk, hoping somehow to nip this new problem in the bud and discovered two things: the actual words being sung were "Who Do You Trust?" and it was a helluva good Thorogood impression. When the image finally stopped spinning and my stomach stopped trying to rebel, it looked like some kind of animal icon lip-synching to the words—a sort of svelte wolf playing air guitar.

"Coyote?" I ventured, speaking the thought as it occurred.

The figure and sound both halted abruptly. Then the icon seemed to take stock of itself.

"Right," it said, still in Thorogood's voice. "Hold on, let me slip into something more comfortable."

The coyote blinked and, as if changing channels, was suddenly a raven, another blink and then a rabbit, a fox, a man with too many legs, a scrawny old gent and, finally, a youth in a toga and winged sandals hovering mid-screen.

"Ah, that's better," he sighed, now sounding more like Zorba the Greek.

"Great, do you do parties?" I asked wryly.

He waggled his brows at me. "Actually, yes, but I prefer the adult kind."

I groaned, really, *really* not in the mood. "Great, I witness one little murder and I get an immortal infestation. Look, you may not be able to tell, but I'm in serious need of my beauty sleep, so if you don't mind—"

"Hey, hey, hey, far as I can tell, aside from the bed wrinkles—" he waved an airy hand at my chest/neck area, "—sleep's been good to you. Besides, I'm a busy man. Messages to carry, mischief to make. It takes effort to make an *entrance*. Least you can do is show some appreciation."

I sighed. If Coyote, or Hermes as he appeared now, was determined to play his little tricks on me, there wasn't a damn thing I could do about it, far as I could tell. Maybe if I just heard him out I could keep things short and sweet.

"Okay, so you have a message for me?" I asked.

"Of sorts," he answered, now studying his cuticles in a pouting sort of way.

"Who do you trust?" I prompted.

He played with a nail that obviously hadn't met his approval.

"Uh huh," he answered vaguely, as if his full attention were elsewhere.

"Great. Do you think you could be any less helpful?"

He glanced up at me reproachfully. "Do you even have to ask?"

"Okay, well, this has been enlightening. Thanks so much for taking time out of your busy schedule—"

I turned back toward my nice warm bed, way too tired for twenty questions.

"Let me ask you something," he demanded casually from the screen behind me. "Do you *really* think the water divinities give a damn about what goes on in Holly-weird?"

My brain must still have been foggy from sleep. The question didn't track.

"What?" I asked, turning back reluctantly, only to find his eyes riveted on the spot where my jammie shirt cut off mid-thigh. I defiantly refused to dive modestly for the covers. Sadly, I didn't think Hermes minded the lack of reaction.

"*Hello*, they're called legs. Not like you've never seen them before. You were saying," I prodded.

"Hmm, yes," he continued, completely unfazed, "I just have to wonder whether they were truly in town to catch the show, you know."

"Is there a message in here somewhere?" I asked, losing patience.

"Somewhere," he agreed. "At least now you know the questions."

Hermes smacked his lips and finally drew his eyes upward to meet mine. "Well, it's been, as you say, enlightening, but—" he smoothed down his toga, which, oh looky there, didn't fit as well as it had previously, "—I must away."

And with the snap of a finger he was whirling around again, shrinking all the while with Def Leppard's "Pour Some Sugar on Me" as his exit music.

All class, that one. I looked toward the bottom of the laptop screen for the time, but it appeared that the power had gone out again with Hermes's departure. Alarm clock flattened, cell phone flatlined, VCR read-out never set, I was dependent on my microwave clock to tell me that it was already nearly ten p.m.

My stomach gurgled loudly, and I realized that the earlier nausea might not owe to vertigo alone, I hadn't eaten in hours or had more than a sip of water with my pain meds. I remembered hearing somewhere that swallowing saltwater would dehydrate a person quickly and I was pretty sure fighting for my life had burned a lot of fuel. I needed nutrients stat.

I sucked down nearly half a bottle of vitamin water from my fridge as I waited for some canned soup to heat and unwrapped a package of saltines. It wasn't gourmet, but it would cover the basics. I barely tasted anything as my brain clicked and whirred over Hermes's cryptic message and Armani's hissy fit—or maybe it was my hissy fit. It was all sort of a blur.

The ringing of my landline barely registered, since hardly anybody even used it besides solicitors and public-opinion pollsters. It wasn't until Christie's voice poured forth from my answering machine that I lurched for the receiver.

"Well, hey," she bubbled, as the click of the line gave me away. "I was just saying that your cell phone seems to be off or something, so I dug out your home number. I thought I might stop by on my way to the club to drop off the proof sheet for my head shots, see what you think."

Bad friend, I scolded myself, *bad, bad friend* forgetting to return Christie's call about getting together. On my behalf, I *had* been a wee bit busy.

The soup and sleep had perked me up, though. In fact, I felt a second wind coming on.

"Christie, I'm so glad you called. You still want company for clubbing?"

Silence resounded. "But you never go with me," she said finally.

"Not true," I answered. "There was the Blue Fish."

"Ye-ah, like, three months ago."

Okay, color me baffled. "If you don't want me to go, why do you keep asking?"

"No, no, no," she gushed, "I *do*, but I bumped into Jack last night at Ondago's and we made plans to meet up at The Kasbah."

"Oh."

"See, that's why I hesitated—I knew you'd give me that 'oh'."

"What? I didn't say a thing."

"Uh huh. You don't say a thing like my grandmother doesn't say a thing, all lips pursed and eyes rolling nearly out of sight."

"Christie, you can't see me! You don't know what I'm doing."

"Okay, what are you doing?" she challenged.

Damn. "Um, well, maybe my lips are a little pursed, but Christie, *Jack?* Half the time he doesn't call. When he does show, he's like an hour late and then acts like you're queen bitch if you've got a problem with that. I just don't get the appeal."

"He can be very charming," she insisted.

"Great. With some substance and a little fairy dust, he might someday be a real boy," I muttered.

"What?"

"Nothing."

"Besides, you sound like you've got a cold or something. You should probably be in bed. I can drop off some chicken soup with the proofs."

"Christie, I'm *not* sick and the last thing I need is more bed rest."

"More?"

"Never mind."

"Okay, something is up. This is totally not like you. I'm not agreeing to anything until you tell me what it is."

Leave it to Christie to be on to me but totally clueless about pretty-boy Jack.

"I want to schmooze."

She snorted. I wouldn't have thought her perky little nose was made for it.

"Really. You're always in the know on the trendy spots. I thought it might be a good idea to listen in for any theories that might be floating around about Circe's death, sift through the gossip."

"Investigate!" Christie breathed the word like it was something wondrous.

"Sort of."

"That's great! Only problem is it's impossible to hear the person across from you, let alone eavesdrop."

I could almost hear Christie chewing her lip, which she did frequently. I thought it was probably the swelling that gave her that Hollywood pout rather than collagen, but I'd never asked.

"Fine, then I'll start conversations. Like I said—schmooze."

"Okay," she answered doubtfully. Her faith in my social skills was heartwarming. "I've just hit your foyer. Buzz me up?"

Foyer, what a nice-sounding word for *empty space between doorways*. Only Christie, I thought, and maybe Jack when he was being snidely *charming* would call it that.

I hit the release button for the main door and let Christie in at her knock, using the intervening time to find clothes. My closet was big on business and workout suits with little in between but some tanks, shorts and concert Ts. Oh, I'd get out for a band I liked—Offspring or the Gorillaz, maybe—but overall, not a big fan of the nightlife, definitely didn't like to boogie. And I'd overgrown the mosh pit years ago the first time I got dropped. Not that *that* crowd went in much for spangles.

Christie took pity on me. "Look, it's not like we've never done this before. Wear something black, which I *know* you have, with a studded belt. We'll go heavy on the eyeliner and mascara, your hoochie-mama red lipstick and you're golden. So the drama."

So fading into the woodwork, I thought. But what the hell, I didn't have any better option.

"Christie, you're a gem. I'll be ready in five."

She waved that off. "Take ten. It's not like anything really gets started until eleven anyway."

"Hey, when did you start using words like hoochie-mama?" I peeked out of the bathroom where I'd taken my clothes to change.

Christie rolled her eyes upward in thought. "I think I stole it from Jesus. Oh, that reminds me, would you show the proofs to him on Monday? I have to get the pictures ordered soon, but I'd like to get his opinion too. He's got a great eye."

I exchanged a look with my reflection in the mirror, nearly freezing myself to stone with mortification. Oh yeah, the gorgon blood was showing. Having fallen asleep with wet hair, it now stuck up and twisted about like writhing snakes. I wasn't sure there was enough mousse in the world to tame it. Ironing would probably take too long.

Fifteen minutes later I thought that *maybe* the club wouldn't bounce me out on my ass. Christie gave me a thumbs-up, which she would have done in any case, but she looked sincere, so I chose to believe it. Hollywood can have that crazy effect of making you care far more about your appearance than you would anywhere else in the world. Insecurity caused maybe by the plethora of the young and beautiful who flooded the place on a regular basis hoping to live the dream.

Yup, La La Land was getting to me. Next thing I knew I'd be churning myself wheat-grass smoothies and practicing extreme yoga.

"Ready to roll," I announced.

Christie neatly bypassed the teeming hordes begging entrance at The Kasbah—Ondago's being *so* last night—by sashaying up to the bouncer and giving him her name. He checked it against his clipboard, eyed me like something the cat had dragged in and grudgingly held the door for us, as if had the decision been up to him, we'd still be cooling our heels.

Made me feel all warm and fuzzy, especially when a cacophony of complaints rose up from the line behind us. Christie smiled graciously at the bouncer on her way past, as if he'd just put her on the path to Oz.

Maybe he had. Even I had to admit that the décor, what I could see of it between bodies, reeked of...well, not the Emerald Kingdom, more jungle cantina. Structural columns looked like trees growing up to the ceiling and spreading into a canopy of leaves that also cascaded down the walls, cut back here and there to expose half-fallen columns, tiki faces and petroglyphs. I half expected to see Indiana Jones come barreling out of the crowd, a rolling boulder of doom bearing down on him.

"Isn't this great?" Christie asked, nearly yelling in my ear.

"It's something," I answered, surprised my throat had recovered enough to achieve volume. "I need a drink. What'll you have?"

Making my way through the crowd was like weaving through rush-hour traffic on a motorbike. There were occasional paths just wide enough to slip through, but you had to be wary of other travelers changing lanes without signaling. By the time I reached the bar, I'd managed to jostle a Colin Farrell look-alike—or maybe even the real thing—and had nearly caught an arm in the face. Once I reached the bar I found I wasn't flashing enough cleavage to rate the bartender's attention until I raised a minor ruckus. I was fully convinced of my own stupidity in coming out by the time I caught up with Christie, who'd waved me over from the midst of a huddle which included, miraculously, Jack I'm-too-sexy-for-my-shirt Moran.

I handed Christie her pink squirrel, which I'd blushed to even order, and slid into the opening that Jack made for me and my already half-finished rum and Coke. The four horsemen of the apocalypse doing water ballet couldn't have shocked me more. *Jack* showing consideration?

Then a woman I'd never seen before gushed directly into my ear, moist breath and all, "Did you *really* fight off Circe Holland's killer?"

Christie gave a weak smile in response to my hard look. "You said you wanted to ask some questions," she shouted from across the circle, "so I had to explain about your investigation."

"What was it *like*?" Jack jumped in.

Ridiculous as it was, I'd not only become the belle of the ball, but I was getting off on it. Or maybe with my depleted electrolytes it was just the drink going to my head. I realized that as in my fortune-telling persona where I pitched my voice low and mysterious, I needed to play a role—the great detective. I regaled them with my edited adventures and quizzed them about rumors and personal knowledge. The fear that the high and mighty would resist talking with an outsider incapable of giving them a leg up in the business dissipated in the face of the great game. I had insider knowledge of the murder. At the moment, that was currency, which seemed to cash out in the form of free drinks, appearing the second I'd polished off the last.

As a third rum and Coke arrived before me a hand descended on my shoulder, sparking a burst of ball lightning which crackled through my body. Silence fell on the group. I knew without turning who had appeared on the scene.

I turned anyway and looked straight up into Apollo's Mediterranean-blue eyes.

"Hello," he said, imbuing it with enough sexuality to give me aftershocks of electricity. "I wonder if I might steal you away for a minute."

Just a minute, my animal brain protested, *not nearly long enough.* Hey, I hadn't said it out loud; my inner censor had to be back online. Go me.

Apollo gave the assembly his twenty-million-dollar smile—or however much he was making per film this year—to make up for taking me away. Hardly a fair trade, I thought, but no one asked me. Anyway, off I went with him, flashing a lame imitation of the movie-star smile.

And off and off into the deepest corner of the jungle bar. Something inside flashed with both excitement and alarm, but I tamped it down. It was all psycho-chemical, I told myself, nothing that couldn't be controlled—if I were asleep or otherwise unconscious.

"I hear you were attacked today," he said, staring deeply into my eyes, radiating concern.

His hands hovered near my upper arms, as if he were about to frisk me to be sure I was intact.

"Wow, good news travels fast in this town. Wanna tell me what I had for breakfast?"

His hands dropped and he looked momentarily to be searching for his motivation.

"How can you be so flip with your life?" he asked. "Perhaps I should have left this to the police. It is too dangerous."

"Is that your way of saying you want me off the case?" I challenged, the alcohol and hormonal imbalance of seconds ago ebbing away.

I studied him for clues, but his face had gone still, as if unsure what emotion to show, he'd just turned off the projector.

"Look, I'm a big girl. I know when to say when. So, if this is about you wanting to express concern and wallow in some misplaced guilt, don't bring me into it. I saw the murder. That's enough to make me a target. On the case, I get to pay my rent while trying to change what is. If this is about the fact that I'm a *girl*—"

"No one who knows Hera would ever call women the weaker sex," he said, sardonic humor reanimating his face.

"Good. Then we're understood. You want to find out what happened to Circe. I want to get paid. It's a win-win situation."

Somehow, he'd gotten even closer without my notice so that if I so much as breathed too deeply my chest would brush his. His lips still quirked in amusement, but that come-hither glint I remembered from our first meeting was back as well.

"Tell me," he ordered, "has anyone ever won an argument with you?"

I thought about it. "Once—"

The word had barely left my mouth when Apollo covered it with his and that torrent of emotion that had earlier ebbed rose up with the force of a tropical storm. Maybe months of deprivation had built my pheromone level to such a point it was bubbling over. It was the only excuse I could think of for my sudden irresistibility. Whatever it was, I was getting swept up in the whirlwind myself. Armani had felt sexy, solid, entirely real. Apollo was like someone else's wet dream, too hot to even think of claiming for my own.

Later, after I snapped to, I might convince myself that it was a combination of the booze and Armani's earlier rejection, but right then I didn't give a damn about anything—the danger of playing with fire, the fact that I was lip-locked in a public place with a *very* public figure. Nothing but the fact that just being pressed up against Apollo's sculpted body was foreplay enough. When his hands brushed my ribs, I nearly squirmed to get them somewhere more effective, already so hot and wet that if he'd decided to take me right up against the wall, I'd have been ready for him.

I'd like to say that when Apollo took my hand and led me out through a side door into a low-lit alleyway that I came to my senses, but Yiayia would have to wash my mouth out with soap. The truth was that I was hormone-poisoned to the point that I was barely aware of anything but the urge to continue where we'd left off. It was the howl of a dog that finally penetrated the erotic haze. I don't know how long the mournful baying had gone on before it registered—a hound dog. Not unheard of, but rare in ultra-urban L.A. Potentially a precious lead on the Strohmeyer case. Then Apollo shifted against me and I almost didn't care. Almost. But that brief lifting of the haze was enough to bring me back to myself.

Damn, I had to be thick or suicidal, or maybe all of the above. I *knew* the stories of Apollo's conquests—the conflicts, the transformations, the illegitimate children, not to mention the funeral pyres.

I had to go. Apollo protested as I pulled away, looking shell-shocked when I stopped him with a raised hand and a shushing. It was hard to hear over my own still-heavy breathing, so I held my breath, attuned myself to the sound.

"I've got to go," I said, once I had the direction down.

"What, because of a *dog*? If it's that damned K—" he bit off whatever he'd been about to say and my knowledge of mythology failed to fill in the blank, but I gave it a pass.

"Look, it's not all about you. This is another case."

I took off like the hounds of hell were chasing me rather than the other way around. Melodramatic, I know. Honey was probably a very nice dog, but still there was that sense of having escaped the fire—the very hot, seductive—dammit, I needed to focus.

For the better part of an hour I tracked the baying hound, but either it was on the move or someone was having a lot of fun at my expense. One final wounded yelp and the sound stopped dead just before midnight. My heart sank even as my abused feet rejoiced. The second wind that had propelled me had died out about twenty minutes into the fruitless chase, and I was ready to collapse.

Tomorrow I'd get back on the phone to the shelters and to animal control to make sure they hadn't forgotten my interest. I'd check in again with the city about new dog licenses. Tonight I planned to fall asleep in my clothes.

I hailed a cab and kept myself awake with self-flagellation. So far I was batting a thousand on this whole PI thing. No doubt if Uncle Christos had stuck around both cases would already be wrapped up with neat little bows. Apollo would have no reason to stick around tempting me to greater heights of stupidity; the company account would be lush. We'd even have money to remodel. Nights like this I cursed him for running off.

Chapter Ten

"Never invoke the gods unless you want them to appear. It annoys them very much."

—G.K. Chesterton, no relation

I hadn't had enough to drink last night to give me a hangover this morning, so I had to be suffering the after-effects of stupidity. That or the fact that my late-afternoon nap had rendered me sleepless until the wee hours of the morning. Anyway, I now had a pounding headache that was even starting to tunnel my vision.

The only upside to my day so far was that Jesus was out on an audition and so not available for snide commentary on the bags beneath my eyes—*so* not Luis Vuitton, darling. God, I'd been around him long enough that I could supply my own put-downs. No physical presence needed.

I groaned as I sat at my desk, head in my hands, praying for the pain meds to kick in and my vision to clear.

When the damned singing fish above my door started talking, it didn't immediately register as anything more than an auditory hallucination, my ears deciding to betray me as well. Slowly, so as not to jar and further pain my head, I looked up, panning only my eyes toward the pesky Pisces. I *knew* I'd taken the batteries out of the damned thing.

"What?" I asked, cranky about feeling foolish.

I don't know what I expected, but it wasn't the deep voice seemingly with its own reverb saying, "We need to talk."

"Look, whoever you are, my head is about to split itself down the center. Whatever you have to say, stick it in a memo. Jesus, if this is some kind of crazy candid-camera thing you're fired."

"I AM POSEIDON, LORD OF THE WATERS AND YOU WILL LISTEN!" the fish boomed, doubling its previous volume.

It felt like someone took a sledgehammer to my head with each word.

"Fine," I said through gritted teeth, "but only if you exercise a little volume control. Otherwise, you're shark bait."

Through the pounding on my brain it was hard to consider what antagonizing the god of the oceans might do to my summer tanning options.

"You will leave my people alone," he commanded, conceding maybe a decibel or two. "We will look to our own."

My left eye twitched. "*Really?* Where the hell were you all yesterday when one of *your own* was trying to put me to sleep with the fishes?"

The rubber fish flapped annoyance. "You did not need our intervention."

"Funny, 'cause from my perspective I was this close—" I demonstrated with my fingers, "—to a watery grave."

"ENOUGH!" the fish bellowed, causing me to wince.

"Oh yeah, this new form of yours—*real* intimidating," I continued, knowing I was pushing my luck, but pissed off and curious about the results all the same. 'Cause that approach had done wonders for the cat. "Maybe if you showed yourself... Though, you fitting the killer's general description and all, maybe there's some reason you don't want to come out and fight like a man."

The only warning I had was a nasty-sounding gurgle-belch before a flood of brackish water exploded forth from the fish's mouth. I jerked back from my desk as if the stream would hit me, then laughed at my own fear. "Ooh, swamp water—very scary!"

And suddenly the flood became a torrent, an entire swollen river bursting its banks. Not so funny after all. Easy enough to run away myself, but my office! Uncle Christos's security deposit!

Something had to be done. I grabbed my desk chair and pulled it with me toward the door, trying to shield my eyes and make progress against the stinging force of the geyser. The chair and I were knocked to the floor once and nearly twice before I managed to get it in place and climb unsteadily aboard. Blinded now by the torrent, I reached for the fish, feeling my way to the mounting, which I ripped from the wall. Plaster rained down on my head and the fish had gone from soaking the rug to soaking me.

The chair keeled over as I jumped down, sprinting toward the outer door with the still-spewing fish like a football player headed for the end zone. I raced down the fire stairs and out into the alleyway.

The flood had trickled to leaky-faucet level and no doubt Poseidon's spirit had long since departed but I took great pleasure in cramming the damned fish into the dumpster where it belonged anyway.

Maybe I'd saved my office, but for the second time in two days I was soaked to the bone and madder than a wet hen.

Pisses me off when my day sounds like a freakin' country-western song.

I squelched my way back to the office to survey the damage and arrange for a wet vac. My nose wrinkled involuntarily at the swamp-water smell of the place. It would be just my luck if the damage seeped down into the office below and I had *two* repair bills to worry about.

At least I kept a change of clothes for myself at the office—I'd say for "just such emergencies", but who the hell anticipated plastic fish gushing pond scum? My life had gotten too damned weird. *I* was the investigator; I was the one supposed to put people in the know. So why the *hell* did I get the feeling that I was the blind man in the game of bluff? It seemed everyone else knew the playing field and gamboled around taunting me, dangling the truth just out of reach.

If there was anyone I should damned well be able to expect straight answers from it was my client. Come hell or high water—oh wait, I'd had near misses on both—he was going to answer my questions. I didn't care if he was akin to Hollywood's crown prince. He'd signed a contract; we'd played tonsil hockey in a club alley. One way or another, I ought to be entitled.

I picked up the office phone and jabbed in his private number from memory. It occurred to me that somewhere in the adrenaline rush to save my office the headache had disappeared. At least something had gone right.

To my surprise, the man of the hour actually answered.

"Hello," he said, voice low and a bit hoarse—I refused to think husky—as if I'd woken him.

"Apollo, it's Tori. We need to have a conversation. *In person.*"

I heard movement. Bed sheets rustling? His throat cleared and he came back to the receiver sounding a bit more normal. "What's happened? You sound upset."

Give that man an exploding cigar, I thought.

"What, you mean you don't *know*? Your freakin' Oracle didn't give you a heads-up on this morning's little visitation?"

"I'll be right there," he said, sounding urgent now, though I couldn't figure out what I'd said that would prompt it.

"Wear old shoes," I suggested, but the receiver had gone dead in my hand.

"I'm in trouble, aren't I?" Apollo asked as I showed him in.

I'd considered meeting with him in Uncle Christos's office, but I had a point to make.

"Big," I agreed, waiting until we'd both squelched across my floor to say anything more.

A comment or question on the moisture wouldn't have been uncalled for but Apollo kept silent, perhaps wisely guessing that it had something to do with my call.

Once we were seated, I pinned him with my very best glare and began. "Let's cut right to the chase. You did not hire me because you thought Circe's death had anything to do with your business. I doubt any of your old crowd gives a damn about the talent agency, and you knew before you even entered my office that we were dealing with one of the divinities. So, you can talk or I can walk, 'cause I've had it up to here—" I held my hand to my hairline, "—with the lot of you right about now." And with myself for not tossing him from my office at the get-go.

His eyes widened, but the only other movement was that of his chest expanding and contracting as he breathed. The seconds ticked by and I relaxed back into my chair, watching his thought process dance over his face—consternation, caginess, resignation. I was pleased with the last. The interview would go so much faster if I didn't have to browbeat Apollo into submission—not that the idea didn't have its perks.

"No," he answered finally. "No one gives a damn about the agency. You want the full story, fine, I'll give you everything I have, but it isn't much. Something odd is going on. Circe is the first death that I know of, but some of the old-timers have gone twitchy and others have seemed to disappear. The oracle has been broadcasting "Get the hell out of Dodge" on all frequencies, and I want to know what the hell is going on. I've worked too hard to get where I am to turn tail and run, even if I had anywhere to go. Since no one on the inside is talking, I've had to go to an outside source."

I'd liked it better when I thought Apollo might have some answers.

"If something's going on in godland, why would you be left out of the loop?"

"Damned if I know. Maybe because I was working with Circe, who no one in their right mind trusts, and got tarred with the same brush. Maybe there's some kind of vendetta thing or war between factions that I'm just not part of. I was up front with you that I want to find out what happened, what Circe was involved in, to be sure I don't get the fallout."

"So what changed your mind?" I asked.

"Excuse me?"

"You didn't show up at the club last night because of my irresistible charm, such as it is. You knew where to find me; you knew about the attack, and you were ready to pull me from the case. Conclusion: you're holding out on me. Care to fill me in?"

Apollo stood abruptly, nearly upending his chair onto the sodden carpet. He filled the room, pacing the six or seven steps the office allowed, but somehow the squishing sound of each footfall diminished the effect.

"If you put others on the spot nearly as well as you do me, you must be a very good investigator. Yes, I went there to fire you. I'd been warned away from investigating Circe's death. Specifically, I'd been told that your life was in danger, but I got the distinct impression last night that pulling my financing wasn't going to take you off the case."

He wasn't looking at me as he said it and something told me there were gaps in the story.

"What else?"

Apollo had stopped in front of my doorway and was eying the twin holes I'd left in the plaster. "You know that headache?" he asked, barely audible with his back to me.

I blinked at the complete non sequitur. "Ye-ah," I answered warily.

"Well, that's kind of a side effect."

"Of what?" My heart rate had kicked up and this time it didn't have anything to do with his proximity per se.

He finally turned, measuring my reaction from there, "A bit of an edge."

"Tell me," I said, already rising to cut off his escape.

"Just a little precog," he answered, holding his ground. "Think of it as your Spidey sense, an early warning system in case of danger. The headache won't last long. It's an effect of waking up pathways in your brain previously closed off. All I did was open some doors."

I stood before him now, hands on my hips, almost a head shorter than him but, I hoped, intimidating in my anger. I put *hold it right there, buster* into my glare. "Without my consent," I stated.

Apollo stayed put, but that could have been his own arrogance. He was a god, after all, what did he have to fear from little ol' me? "Yes."

No apologies, not the least abashed. Okay, on the one hand, I could see how a little precognition might not be such a bad thing. On the other, I knew that Apollo's gifts did not come free, and I didn't like the idea that he could play with my mind at will. It hadn't turned out so well for Cassandra, prophetess of Troy, when Apollo's broad shoulders failed to make her swoon. Oh sure, she still had the visions, but no ability to make anyone believe. All she could do was watch the horrible reality unfold. Something like that would drive me barking mad. I wasn't feeling too far from that ledge as it was.

We continued our standoff, toe-to-toe, me with my anger and Apollo with his defiance, daring me to take issue.

"Thank you," I said with effort. "Don't ever mess with my head again." I tried to drive the point home with my glare.

Apollo's head jerked fractionally. "You want to tell me about the carpet?" he asked, changing the subject.

"I'm not finished with you yet. *Who* threatened me?"

"The same god, I presume, who's responsible for your water damage."

"Poseidon?"

He nodded. "Do you think he's the killer?"

"No. My attacker and Circe's were one and the same. If it had been Poseidon who'd grabbed me, I doubt I'd still have a pulse. How much do you trust Hephaestus?"

That one shocked him. Apollo's eyes met mine. "Hiero? Last I checked, he was neither green nor scaly. What's he got to do with anything?"

"The place I was attacked yesterday—he's the one who pointed it out on the map. No one else knew where I'd be."

"But if it had some significance to your case, it wouldn't have been too hard to figure out."

Damn, all that beauty and brains too. My righteous anger was wearing off and with it went my defense against Apollo's spell. I had to end this quickly.

"Okay, point for you," I conceded. "Sorry to get you down here in such a rush."

Double uh oh. The smolder was back in his eyes. He must have sensed the second the mood had shifted.

Apollo reached out to me, and I backed out of my own office in retreat.

"Here, let me get the door for you," I offered

It was a lame cover and we both knew it. Before making his exit, he stopped to take my chin and force me to meet his eyes.

"You had your chance, you know. Off the case and out of my—clutches. I think you know what will happen if we continue working together."

I struggled to remember why that was a very bad thing; I fought to dredge up some anger at his arrogance, but deep down I both feared and hoped he was right.

"Is this where you start twirling your mustachios?" I asked, trying to dispel the mood.

"If you insist on playing the damsel in distress. Fortunately for me, I don't think your police detective is much of a challenge."

Urk. It was on the tip of my tongue to protest, but everything I could think to say would come out as admission or encouragement. I didn't see how he could really *know* anything and certainly didn't want to give him any fuel for the fire. The gods weren't known for their charity toward the competition. Besides, Armani was clearly *not* mine in any way, shape or form.

That fact was illustrated beautifully a few hours later when Lau called to inform me brusquely that my presence was requested at the precinct to once more go over my story of Circe's murder and discuss "any subsequent attacks". If Armani had thrown me to the wolf, then he was probably still in a snit about yesterday.

I agreed to come in for two reasons. One, I didn't trust Lau not to find some way to force the issue, and that would provide her with way too much satisfaction. Two, given the site of yesterday's momentous battle with the Creature from the Black Lagoon, I wasn't entirely convinced that Circe's murder wasn't tied in some way to the actress's death. I still wanted to get a look at the Talbot file. Not that Lau would slip it to me, of course, but it might be possible to tap into one of Uncle Christos's police contacts of yore.

Besides, there wasn't much to do on my other investigation but wait for my various phone calls to be returned. I was particularly anxious to hear from the widow whether she knew of anyone in the Sunset Strip area to whom her husband might have gone, dragging the dog behind him. With any luck, I'd close the case by sundown. Funny enough, clients were so much happier to pay when you'd actually gotten results. Not necessarily faster, you understand, just less grudging.

Lau kept me cooling my heels for a good half hour, so I decided that when she was ready, she could come find me. Meanwhile, it seemed only polite to drop in on Christos's old drinking buddies and see what they were up to. Stan Muldavi was out on a call, but I was in luck for George Santos and Tony Robbins, who were catching up on paperwork. Neither noticed me until I snuck up behind George and covered his eyes.

He practically jumped out of his skin, but I kept my hands in place.

Tony chuckled. "You're getting old, George. Ten years ago you wouldn't let some slip of a thing sneak up on you."

George could shrug me off in a second if he chose. Instead, he asked, "Is she cute?"

"Nah. Kinda buck-toothed and cross-eyed."

"Tori?"

I pulled my hands back. "Very cute, you two. You ought to take your show on the road."

"Can't—George gets carsick. Hey, you heard anything from your uncle?"

"Yeah," George chimed in. "Tell him he owes me money."

"Great. That'll certainly get him back here," I answered. "Listen, I've got a question; I was hoping one of you might have heard something."

"If it's about the Circe Holland homicide—" Tony made a warding sign.

"Not that. I've got this missing dog case. The woman's husband took off and their hound seems to have followed him—or maybe been dog-napped. Anyway, the lady figures good riddance to the husband, who was catting around, but she'd like the dog back. The only problem is that I probably have to find the former to get the latter and the husband's pulled a vanishing act. I'm wondering if you guys have anything on him, like some legal reason he skipped town or maybe he's on the sheets for a domestic dispute."

Tony shrugged. "Christos will be so glad to hear his business is going to the dogs. What's the deadbeat's name?"

"Dick Strohmeyer."

George and Tony shared a Look.

"What?"

It was George's turn to shrug. "Go ahead, tell her. Can't hurt."

I pushed some files aside to perch on the edge of George's desk. "I'm all ears."

Tony settled back in his chair. "Strohmeyer's girlfriend was in last week, calling for the wife's head on a platter. She talked to Nelson, but half the squad room heard her."

"Yeah, real spitfire," George contributed.

"And easy on the eyes, but that mouth—eesh. Anyway, she hadn't seen Dick in days. The wife claimed he moved out, but the girlfriend wasn't buying it. She thinks the wife, your client, had him whacked."

I couldn't see Annette Strohmeyer whacking anybody. 'Course, I couldn't see her getting all sappy over a slobbery hound, but it was always the ones you least expected.

"Did Nelson take her seriously?"

"Don't know. He talked to her for a good long time. Certainly wrote down all her particulars."

Tony's eyes flicked past me.

I turned to look. Uh oh.

"Can you get me her name and address?" I asked sotto voice.

"Call you later," he said quickly. "Detective Lau, pleasure to see you."

"Robbins, Santos," she answered with a bare nod. "*You.* We have an appointment."

As if I'd kept *her* waiting. I bid farewell to the guys and followed Lau, past her desk, which always creeped me out with its array of desiccated sea life—mounted piranha, urchin shells, starfish—in lieu of photographs, into one of their stark interview rooms.

Lau practically slammed the door behind me and ordered me to sit. The solitary table was littered with files, as if the detective had commandeered the room for some time and had made herself comfortable.

"Why did you fail to report your attack?"

"Huh?" I asked, honestly baffled. "You mean the fish?"

Lau crossed her arms over her chest and leaned against the door, pointedly, if one could be said to lean pointedly. "Armani's not here to run interference for you, and I've got all the time in the world. You can tell me and go free to overcharge some poor schmuck for your time or you can sit here pissing me off until I lock you up for withholding evidence."

"*What evidence?*" I nearly shouted. "It's a freakin' plastic fish. You want to go dumpster diving, you be my guest."

"What the *hell* are you babbling on about?" she asked.

I stared. "What the hell are *you* talking about?"

"Yesterday. Venice Beach. Ring any bells?"

Oh, that. That was, like, ages ago. Since then I'd been kissed, threatened, flooded and whammied with a spankin' new psychic power. Surely I could be forgiven for forgetting a little near-death experience.

"Oh."

"Yeah, oh. Now, what's this about your dumpster?" Lau's eyes narrowed on me.

"First, I wasn't attacked at the beach. I slipped and the shock of the cold water knocked me out."

"Uh huh." Oh, it sounded like agreement, but read more like giving me enough rope to hang myself.

"Second, the damned fish in the dumpster was someone's idea of a practical joke, rigging the singing fish above my door to give me a dunking." I squelched a dribble of water out of my shoes onto the industrial carpet for effect. Unlike my spare suit, the shoes hadn't been hung above the waterline.

"First, Mr. Lafferty—you remember him—your rescuer—claims that you were struggling against someone."

"How did you—"

The canary-eating cat had never smiled so broadly. "Armani tracked him down when he figured you were holding out. Wait, let me guess, you got your foot caught, maybe in your mouth?"

I seriously didn't like this woman. "I'm not under any obligation to report a struggle." Of course, an *assault*, being a crime, was another matter and I didn't think Lau was the type to be put off by semantics.

"You do if it had anything to do with my murder investigation."

I was all out of smart-ass comments. If Lau could convince a judge that I was withholding evidence, obstructing justice, my PI license would be suspended. Suspended, hell, I could be facing jail time. Of course, if my license was pulled it was only a matter of time before I got arrested anyway for vagrancy. Blacklisted from the circus, blackballed by the police, I'd be a two-time loser. It wasn't as if I had another Uncle Christos waiting in the wings to bail me out.

"What on earth would I gain by keeping quiet about the attack?"

114

"You tell me. Why did you let the killer get away in the first place?"

My eyes nearly bugged out. "Are you kidding me? Did you see what that guy did to Circe? I'd gone in for a simple delivery. *Unarmed.* How the hell was I supposed to stop him?"

"One of the witnesses said that you had the murderer by the arm and you released him."

But I heard what she wasn't saying. "What about the *other* witnesses?"

Lau's lips compressed into a thin line. I thought I even heard the gritting of teeth. "Why do you think I didn't haul you in sooner? It starts to look pretty suspicious, though, in light of the new unreported attack." I opened my mouth to renew my protest, but she plowed right on. "Don't even try to tell me that there's no connection. You were investigating the death of that actress, one of Circe Holland's clients, who, by the way, drowned. Who are you protecting?"

"Drowned!" I was on the edge of my seat. "I knew that she died in the bath, but I was thinking drugs," *or drained life force, per the dragon lady's contract.*

I looked down at the files spread before me and caught the names Holland and Talbot. Everything I needed was here. I wondered if I dared use my gorgon mojo on the great detective.

It was a huge risk. If I locked the door, anyone trying to enter would get suspicious. If I left it unlocked, anyone could walk in. Plus, as far as I knew, Lau could see and hear perfectly well while frozen and I would be in deep doo-doo when she unfroze.

I was an idiot. As soon as I admitted to myself that I had the power, I should have experimented, tested duration, the ability to snap someone out of it at a moment's notice. Now I was stuck. This might be my only chance to get at those files since it seemed I'd turned Armani against me—and I didn't even want to think about how much that hurt.

Lau had been watching me closely, so it was no trick at all to catch her eyes. "Freeze," I said, quietly but firmly.

I waited for her to ask me what the hell I was doing, but except for the subtle motion of her chest expanding and contracting she was as still as a statue—the kind farmers used to frighten off crows. I wasted no time in rifling through the files.

Circe's autopsy report was fascinating. Clearly the ME had been baffled by the lack of apparent aging. Whatever magical treatments Circe had been giving herself at the cost of other people's lives had even repaired the usual dental wear. Unless the victim had survived on an all-liquid diet, it was inconceivable that her teeth should be as good as new. The ME would probably be dining out on the story of Circe's oddities for months—names carefully excised, of course.

Lau might unfreeze at any moment and even though I could freeze her again, every second that ticked by brought the risk of discovery. I flipped quickly to Sierra Talbot's file and skimmed through, getting caught up here and there, mostly on the roommate's interview. Tracy Challis, whose address and phone number I memorized in case I needed to talk to her later, had suspected Sierra of having a stalker. Sierra never said so directly, she admitted, but just before she died she'd suddenly become determined to move back to Ohio. She'd finally landed a real role, kick-starting her career. It seemed so odd... *Unless*, I thought, *she'd gotten the "get out of Dodge" memo.* Did that tie her to Apollo and/or his oracle, I wondered. Or did she have inside information on the source of the danger?

The doorknob twisted. Fear hit the plunger on a shot of adrenaline, which raced through my system. I stood and clapped loudly in the second it took the door to swing open—only to be blocked by Lau's unmoving back. The paralysis held and I was SOL.

"What the hell?" Armani asked.

I quickly rounded the table to try again with Lau, while Armani gave the door another push, rocking her forward. She was going to have one hell of a bruise.

"Unfreeze," I said, going for force without volume. Nothing. "Release," I tried.

Armani hit the door again, this time with his full weight behind it and Lau fell forward into my arms, throwing me back against the table while I braced myself to hold her stiff dead weight. Armani bolted into the room, only to be brought up short when he spotted me pinned beneath his partner's frozen form.

"What did you do?" he asked, rushing forward to take her from me. "Helen, Helen, can you hear me?"

He looked around for somewhere to lay her down, but there wasn't enough floor space and she was too stiff for the chairs. He ended up holding her awkwardly, torn between watching her with concern and glaring me down.

"What the *hell* did you do to her? Neurotoxin? Hypnosis? What?"

I was flummoxed. "Thanks. I really appreciate your faith. You're not going to believe this, but all I did was tell her to freeze."

"That's it," Armani made as if to yell for backup.

"Wait, wait, wait!" I begged desperately. "I'll prove it to you." *Stupid moronic idiot*, I berated myself. "Look at your watch."

I don't know why he did it. If he'd been me, I probably would have locked him up and thrown away the key.

"Got the time?" I asked.

"It's—"

"Freeze." I put very little force behind it, still fearful about what I'd done to Lau and why she hadn't snapped to. Too much of a good thing, I guessed. If it weren't for the fact that I could see her breathing...

Armani stopped—for about a minute, probably the longest one of my life.

"Eleven forty—wait, that's not right."

"You lose a minute?" I asked.

Armani stared at me as if at some kind of alien being, full of fear and awe and *questions*, so many questions, the first of which was, "How?"

But as he said it, Lau started to slump and he was distracted getting her into a chair.

"Helen, you all right?"

She wasn't verbal yet. Her muscles sagged, but were not yet under her control. A full-on panic attack threatened to pound my heart to the breaking point. What would the police do to me? Had I hurt her? If the paralysis of voluntary muscles was this complete, had I killed the man/god I'd struggled with yesterday? He could seemingly breathe underwater, but what if, like a shark, he had to keep moving in order to do so?

Armani pinned me with his gaze. "Bring her around."

I collapsed into the second visitor's chair. "I don't know how," I answered weakly. "I think she'll be okay in just a minute."

Circe's minion had only halted for a moment when I'd given him the Look. It must have been that belief or vocalization or something gave it more force. I was horrified at myself and half-ready to swear off using my power for good and all.

Lau rolled her head in the next instant to find me. "What—?" she asked.

"You fainted."

"Fainted, hell," Armani exploded. "She—"

Lau shook her head faintly. "Wanna hear—" she sucked in a jagged breath, "—from her."

"Would you believe gorgon blood?" I asked.

Her chest rose and fell suddenly in a staccato motion and I feared she'd gone into cardiac arrest. It took me a full five seconds to realize she was laughing.

"Damn that hurts," she said finally. "Welcome to the sisterhood."

Chapter Eleven

"I don't want to see your face again—unless it's on a milk carton."

—*Lenny Rialto, second generation, Rialto Bros. Circus*

You could have knocked me over with a feather.

"Huh?" I asked cleverly.

She gave a half-bow from her chair. "I am a direct descendent of Liu Lei."

"I'm sure that should mean something to me, but I have to confess—"

"Damn Eurocentric country," Lau said, back to her irascible self as she cut me off. "Liu Lei, *the dragon tamer.*"

Clear as mud. "Um."

Lau rolled her eyes. "Reader's Digest version—Liu Lei, born during the Xia Dynasty with the ability to tame and ride dragons, given charge of King Kong Jia's four beasts. Unfortunately, one died in his care. Not his fault; if it's a dragon's time to go, there's nothing anyone can do about it. His dishonor was being too cowardly to come forward. Anyway, the family fell out of royal favor," which I guessed was a euphemism for *was forced to flee the country,* "but the ability continued to breed true."

She hadn't laughed at me—well, okay, she had. Still, I was pretty sure if I laughed back I'd be donkey dust. I looked at Armani to see how he was taking things. Shell-shocked might be understating matters.

"So, you're a dragon tamer," I asked, just for clarification.

Lau huffed, sensing the skepticism behind the question. "More like guardian these days. Most of the creatures have their heads in the sand, hoping we're just an evolutionary mistake that will pass like all the rest. They have a different conception of time, being immortal and all. Meanwhile, they dream of fat prey and no men around to hunt them into extinction."

"How do you know what they dream?"

"Who do you think spins the fantasies that lull them to sleep? It's what we do, speak to them in pictures, soothe them mind-to-mind."

"Uh huh." I took a seat of my own. "So, ah, where's this dragon you're watching?" It was well past breakfast, but I wasn't sure how many more impossible things I could take. Maybe the caffeine and sugar deprivation actually helped in that department.

Armani cut in before she could answer. "Hold up. What the hell kind of drugs did you give her?"

Great, we were back to that. Feel the love.

"Underground," Lau said, ignoring him. "Earthquakes are the dragon rolling over."

I was afraid I was going to break our tentative rapport by bringing up, oh, I don't know, *tectonic plates* and a little thing called geology, but Armani beat me to it.

"You're both insane. Helen, I'm getting you checked out. *You*," he said, pointing to me, "are staying right here."

"Nick," Lau said, making me bristle at the use of Armani's first name. "Sit. Before we start talking about crazy, why don't we let Ms. *Gorgonz*ola here speak?"

So much for rapport.

"Listen, b—" I caught the word before it actually left my mouth, "—babe, you're starting to tick me off, so unless that dragon of yours is ready to play second, you might not want to issue me a challenge."

Armani growled to get us back on track.

"*Fine*. I'm just saying you've already seen what I can do. So far, Ms. Dragon Whisperer is all talk." Okay, the name she'd come up with was way better. So sue me. "*Anyway—*" gods, where did I start? "—it's like this…"

I told them. Everything—the attacks, the hints of a divine comeback, old ones like Yiayia's contact afraid to talk for fear of retribution—everything but the fact that Apollo himself was very likely *that* Apollo, which I figured was his business. By the end of my recitation, Armani had gone a whiter shade of pale and, lacking a third guest chair or the power to make it to the one at his desk, had collapsed onto his butt in an unceremonious heap. He rallied as I wound down.

"So, to recap, Circe is—or was—a psycho who believed some crazy contract clause prolonged her life. Sierra Talbot may or may not have had a stalker but either way was ready to blow her big break. Apollo believes some psychic when she says to bug out of L.A. and you and Helen believe gods and dragons walk the earth. Have I got the basics?"

Lau and I exchanged a look. "In a nutshell," she agreed.

Armani raked a hand through his hair and left it standing straight up.

"What the hell kind of psychoactive chemicals have you two been smoking? I might expect this kind of craziness from Tori, but you, Helen—what the hell?"

Lau stiffened and I could almost see the stick up her butt snap back into place as she rose from the table. "Let's go."

"Where?" Armani asked suspiciously.

"A little road trip. I'll let the evidence speak for itself. In the meantime, you might not want to say anything more you're going to regret later on."

I think I could have knocked Armani over with a feather right then, and after his comment about what could be expected from me, I was sorely tempted, but it would hardly have been sporting.

No one spoke as Lau marched us off to her car. Armani took point, leaving me to sit in the back like a prisoner, half wondering if everyone in the world hid behind a façade of normalcy. But no, Armani was way too flummoxed to be hiding a mind-bending secret of his own. I wouldn't be taking bets on anyone else any time soon.

Tension was our co-pilot for the long, windy trip up Beachwood Drive toward the top of Mount Lee. After a while, Armani reached over to flick the radio on and messed with the knob until he found a classic rock station. Heart's "Magic Man" filled the silence, but the way my love life was going I didn't want to think about magic hands or anything of that nature, so I watched the scenery, putting two and two together.

"You've got to be kidding me—the dragon sleeps under the Hollywood sign!"

"More or less," Lau agreed primly.

"Unbelievable."

"I should have my head examined for not locking you both up," Armani growled.

Lau took her attention away from the road to cut him a withering look. "Judgment in advance of the evidence?"

"The evidence of my life to date suggests that dragons don't exist. If they did there'd be reported sightings right along with Bigfoot and UFOs."

"Are you saying *those* are real?" she fired back.

They squabbled all the way to the summit—like siblings, I thought. It made me smile. Finally, we pulled off, having gone as far as we could go but still some distance from the Hollywood sign.

"You can't see him," Lau explained as we exited the car. "He's curled up in a hollow within the mountain."

"Do you have to be this close to, you know, um, work with him?" I asked.

"It's easier the closer I am, but no. I can't be too far as the crow flies, within about a ten-mile radius, I'd guess, but I don't have to be right on top of him. This is for your benefit."

With that she stalked off across the nearly pristine hillside and chose a nice thick patch of grass on which to strike a meditative pose. Lotus, I thought it was called, but it had been years since my aborted yoga experience. Kickboxing was way more my speed.

Armani alternately prowled the hillside like a great cat on patrol and shot searching glances at his partner. Me he avoided looking at entirely, until the ground suddenly shifted beneath our feet, shuddered, sending rocks skittering and dropping us to our knees before settling to absolute stillness. His startled gaze flew to mine then, as if to assure himself it really had happened.

I was betting my eyes were the size of saucers. I hadn't had much chance to consider whether I believed she could do it at all, but I certainly hadn't thought it would be so immediate.

"So?" she asked smugly, still sitting back on her heals amidst the grass.

A weird tremor took hold of me, like an echo of the heaving earth, but it came with an injection of adrenaline. Apollo's early warning system?

"So?" a new voice echoed Lau, shimmering into view before us like a cartoon mirage. Only the figure before us was never meant to form human speech—a fox-like muzzle, hell, a fox-like body, glowing like golden flame in the sunlight. Only its size, more husky than fox, and its whipcord serpent's tail indicated that this was something other.

"Hermes?" I asked tentatively.

"Iemisch, actually," he answered, strutting forward and lashing his tail dramatically. "I wore it just for you, being that you're looking for dragons and all."

Heck of an early warning system, I thought. I'd hardly had time to blink before Hermes's appearance. I wondered whether it was a flaw in Apollo's "gift" or whether the understatement of the tremor was commentary on the danger level.

"Uh huh. Why is it that everyone seems to know my business before I do?"

The fox-thing dipped his head in lieu of a shrug. "Damned if I know. Could be the bugs."

I couldn't help it—I immediately ran my fingers over my lapels and jacket seams, looking for odd lumps. I assumed the fox's bark-chirp was a laugh at my expense.

"Okay, Mr. Smartypants, what's the story?"

He did another dip-shrug. "Here Be Dragons."

"Look, Iemisch, Hermes, whoever you are, I love banter as much as the next gal, really, but we've got a case to solve, and I'm pretty sure the detectives here would like to clock out sometime today. So, if you don't have anything helpful for us, like a treasure map straight to the baddies with evidence tied up in a neat bow, we've really got to get going."

I looked to Lau and Armani for backup, but I wasn't sure either had heard a word I'd said. Armani had frozen as if he'd just had a Eureka! moment and Lau watched him as if she could rip the thought straight out of his head.

"What?" Hermes and I asked at once.

Armani turned slowly but didn't say anything for a moment, maybe going over things again. "We don't need him. I think I've got it."

The fox's lips pulled back in a snarl. "Do tell."

Armani looked at me and, as always, my heart gave that stutter-jump it was so fond of. This time because even with the others there it was me he focused the explanation on. "If you were going to stage a coup, why would you do it so far from the seat of power?"

"It depends what kind of power you're concerned with—the almighty dollar, fame, influence. L.A. isn't exactly the back of beyond," Lau sniped.

But I thought I could see where he was going. "Because it has to be here, doesn't it?" he asked the fox.

And all of a sudden all the pieces snapped into place. I called myself a thousand times a fool. "They're going to flex their magical muscles by dropping us into the drink!"

"I think so. Sierra Talbot's fear, the Oracle's warning—it all makes sense."

"No, it doesn't," Lau countered, raining on our parade. "Why kill Sierra? Who would have believed her?"

"In these crazy days when we see a terrorist hand in every abandoned bag, you've got to be kidding. She wouldn't have to mention gods, even if she knew what she was dealing with. All she'd have to do is give a credible-sounding tip on a terrorist plot. It's speculation, sure, but work with me. The fact that rather than move up the plan, someone took Sierra out means they probably had some reason to wait. Maybe a day of significance. Maybe—"

Hermes's jaws snapped in irritation. "Well, I know when I'm not wanted. That's the last time I waste a killer entrance." He turned tail, which whipped angrily behind him.

"Wait!" I yelled, remembering that earlier warning shudder. "Whose side are you on anyway?"

He swung his head back around and fixed his inhuman eyes on mine. "I haven't decided yet. Whichever wins, I suppose, though with the forces arrayed against you—" he shook his head sadly, "—it will hardly make for a decent match."

"Then tell us something that will even things out."

"And risk the wrath of my fellows?" He turned away again, this time with an air of finality. "No, you do not seem to be stuck for a solution. I will take my leave."

He paced away, growing less material with each step until the gently swaying grass could be seen right through his form. Finally, he was gone altogether, though the strains of the Steve Miller Band floated back to me on the breeze, "*—and fly to the revolution.*"

"I must be crazy. I'm starting to believe this whole thing," Armani said, staring at the place where Hermes had vanished.

"Just starting?" I asked. "I'd say the mark of a wise, *sane* man is an open mind willing to adjust as circumstances dictate."

Lau eyed us sourly. "I hate to interrupt this little love fest, but I have an idea of what might be taking the gods so long to set things in motion."

"So you're with us on that now?" Armani asked.

She shrugged. "As a wise, sane woman," she mocked, "it makes as much sense as anything I can come up with."

"Okay then—shoot."

"Explosives. Tori says the gods have lost a lot of their power. What if they need something to start things off with a bang—a concentration of energy they can magically amplify? In any reaction, most of the energy goes into jump-starting the process, so if they can do that artificially..."

"Oh my gods!" I stared at her in horror. "And something like that is going to take time and care to collect without raising any red flags."

"Bingo."

"But I know just the man to do it." Both detectives stared at me. "Hiero Cholas, a.k.a. Hephaestus, god of all things technological. How hard do you think it would be for a special effects guru to lay hands on the right stuff?"

Silence reigned.

On the way back to the station we plotted. Armani and Lau were taking point on the explosives angle, since any interest I showed would get me on a Federal watch list, not to mention likely be completely unproductive. They were also going to find some way to get Hiero tailed, even if they had to do it themselves. I had dibs on Sierra's roommate and Circe's long-ignored files.

Earlier leap of my heart aside, I still had several bones to pick with Armani, but I was sure right up until the time that he put a hand on my arm to hold me outside while Lau proceeded us in that I wasn't going to get the chance.

The breeze blew my unruly curls into my face as I stood there waiting for him to begin. He watched the curls, but declined to brush them romantically from my face, preferring to watch me spit hair out of my mouth.

"Very sexy, Karacis," he commented.

There were days I considered hacking the whole mop to within an inch of its life, but I had a feeling that arming me with sheers right now would be a bad idea.

"Just say what you have to say," I snapped.

"I'm sorry for what I said before." Points to him for actually holding eye contact and projecting sincerity.

"Which part? The part where you accused me of drugging your partner or the part where you were going to lock me up?"

That made him look away.

"Oh, and what about the part where you investigated me to begin with?"

"I was worried about you. I had no idea Lau was going to call you in for questioning."

"But you ratted me out."

Armani's eyes rose to meet mine again. "I passed on information pertinent to an ongoing investigation, yes."

"And you're just a poor automaton, slave to your rules and regulations? That's some defense."

"I'm not going to apologize for doing my job."

"Fine."

I started to walk past him, but he, thankfully, stopped me with a hand to my arm. "Dinner?"

"Is that your way of dodging an apology?"

"Just answer the question," he growled.

"Your treat?" I asked.

He nodded.

"Nice place, real utensils?"

I could tell by the look on his face that I was pushing it, but he nodded again.

"One condition, though, that puts us even. We drop the whole thing. Deal?" he asked.

Guess he could see me milking it for all it was worth. Hmm. It was a tough call—a free meal/almost date versus something to hold over Armani. If I really worked at it, I could probably find a way to keep the agreement and still tweak him.

"Okay," I agreed finally, "but no seafood."

Circe's files were a complete waste of time. There were no helpful death threats like: "Dear Circe, It would be my greatest honor to see you dead. If it's not too inconvenient for you, I've chosen the alleyway behind Renee's, the better to chance witnesses to your downfall. Signed, Third God to the Left." Oh no, that would have been too easy. If I hadn't already ruled out a fully human perp, I'd now have a solid list of mortal suspects, A-, B- and C-list actors who had to be pleased as punch by Circe's early shuffle off the mortal coil. However, since I'd seen most of them on screen at one time or another, I was pretty certain they lacked a certain scaly green quality.

I'd left a message for Sierra Talbot's roommate earlier, but it hadn't been returned—or if it had, the message had gone to my dearly departed cell phone or my office answering machine. Unfortunately, we still used Uncle Christos's antiquated model, so there was no way for me to check messages remotely. Since Sierra and Tracy's apartment was in West Hollywood, a helluva lot closer to Circe's office than mine downtown, I decided just to swing by and hope Tracy was in.

I sat outside in the Camaro for a minute just getting a feel for the neighborhood, watching the flow. There wasn't a ton of foot traffic. A young mother in spandex prepared to power walk with her sleeping child strapped to her chest in what looked like a reverse backpack; a twenty-something guy wrestled an oversized package through the front doors. I emerged to help him, but he was already through and gone by the time I reached the entrance.

Once there I was confronted with an entire panel of buttons numbered but with no corresponding names. If you didn't know the apartment number of the party you'd come to see you didn't belong. I chose the correct button and waited for a distorted voice to "Yes?" me through the intercom.

"Tori Karacis," I answered the disembodied voice, "I called earlier about Sierra T—"

A buzzer sounded and a click came from the inner door. I took that as my welcome.

The woman who watched me approach from the doorway to apartment 6D was a surprise. For some reason, I'd expected Sierra's roommate to be another struggling actress, but I didn't get that vibe from Tracy. She stood all of about five foot two in her bare be-ringed feet, cutoffs and dashiki. Her RuPaul blonde hair hung in dreadlocks halfway down her back. Her bronzed face was unadorned except for bars through her left brow, nose and lower lip.

"Hey," she said, studying me rather than inviting me in. "I'm sorry I didn't call you back earlier. I just—couldn't deal. Plus, I already told the police everything."

I nodded sympathetically.

"So you, like, have some ID?"

I flashed my PI license and tried not to stare at her hardware while she looked it over.

"Okay then, come on in." Finally, she stepped aside, admitting me to her inner sanctum, where I nearly choked on the clashing potpourri of scents duking it out inside.

Impressions formed through the haze—artwork on the walls tending toward stark silhouettes and simple but somehow compelling pictures in bold colors. Beyond those minimalist scenes the design seemed like something out of India— sumptuous fabrics, a three-quarters life-size statue of a multi-armed goddess, an elephant-headed god staring down from a bookshelf.

"The motif was mostly Sierra's," Tracy said, having turned and noticed my distraction. She ran her hand over a satin pillow on their low-slung couch. "The pictures are mine, though."

"They're wonderful."

Tracy sighed heavily and met my gaze. "Thanks. I don't suppose you've got any connections in the art world?"

"Afraid not."

"Yeah, well. Have a seat, please. Can I get you anything? I've got mango iced tea."

"That would be great."

The cloying scents were starting to give me that tickly itchy sensation in my throat that I got in smoky bars. A tingle crept up my nose, and I looked hurriedly around for a tissue. None in sight. As a last resort, I flung my hand up before my face just in time to let out a King-Kong-sized sneeze. I never had been dainty, but thankfully it was more noise than funk.

"Sorry," Tracy called from the little kitchenette off to the right. "Sierra never would let me burn the stuff inside. She didn't want to smell—well, *reek* she called it. But I had to chase away, you know, all the negative energy."

"Sure," I said, like I got it. The stuff would sure chase me out.

"I'll open up a few windows in a minute."

She came back with two tall glasses of mango iced tea with raw sugar granules still spinning at the bottoms and handed me one. I sipped mine gratefully while she propped a window open with a wedge.

"They fall again the second you let them go," she explained, relaxing all the way back into a covered chair. "So, what do you want to know?"

"This stalker that Sierra had, what can you tell me about him?"

"Nothing. I'm not even sure there was one. Sierra mentioned some guy early on in the shoot. Strange. Kind of intriguing, but *strange* was kinda how she put it. Then she'd move on to talk about the film and how the water was so cold that her nipples puckered right up but that she didn't know how anyone would ever tell them from the goose bumps. Sierra was a chatterer. I'd perk up at words like guy and nipples, weird stuff like that, though mostly—" she shrugged. "You know."

She said that a lot. Verbal shorthand willing me to agree so she could commute her words. Not a talker like her roommate.

"What about her decision to leave? Did she talk about that?"

Tracy sat up from her slump to wrap her hands around her sweating glass of tea and bring it to her lips. Once she set it down again, she practically burst from her chair to prowl the apartment. I wondered if it was nerves or if she wasn't a sitter either. More like a perpetual motion machine.

"She did, but she was pretty vague, you know, like a newspaper horoscope. She just kept saying that something bad was going to happen and that we had to get out. L.A. was a death trap. I asked her what she'd been smoking." She whipped around to me. "She didn't, by the way. Sierra was as clean-cut as they come. One of those—oh, what do they call themselves?—straight-edge people. My body is my temple and all that."

"Go on," I prodded when she came to an abrupt halt, the suspicion of tears glimmering in her eyes.

"Well, that's the strange thing. Sierra wasn't exactly the credulous type, you know. All these statues, she just liked the look of them. It wasn't a religious thing, but she ranted about the end of L.A. like she'd just seen the four horsemen of the apocalypse with her own eyes. She even had me spooked. Not that I have anywhere else to go."

Tracy rubbed her arms vigorously. "I'm going to close that window again."

She stayed at the window even after it was secured, staring out.

I had the feeling she was pulling herself together, but I had to plow on.

"She wasn't suicidal?"

A choked laugh escaped her. "Scared yes, crazy maybe, but not suicidal. She was talking about heading to New York, taking a run at Broadway."

Tracy's head fell against the window to rest. A second later her stillness changed, set.

"What is it?" I asked.

"Damn freaks."

Holy non sequitur. "Um, come again?"

"Those smarmy 'Death Site' tours. A week dead and they've already added Sierra to the route. Some of the freaks come back on their own."

I joined Tracy at the window and followed her gaze to the man on the street. Fedora pulled low, collar high. A tingle shivered over me; goose bumps raised the hair on my arms. I somehow doubted that was Sam Spade down there keeping the place under surveillance.

"I'll talk to him," I promised. In fact, I looked forward to the confrontation now that we were on my turf, terra firma, rather than his. On my way to the door I dropped a card on Tracy's coffee table. "Call me if you remember anything or if he shows again."

Adrenaline coursing through my system, I took the stairs rather than wait for the elevator. I still hadn't practiced my damned stare, so I did what I could in the rush down to focus and hone my anger, the better to whammy him the second our eyes met. I hit the street with a full head of steam, flying at Circe's killer like a Fury on speed—until his head snapped up and he and his mirrored sunglasses met me head-on.

Instantly, my limbs petrified. The very blood in my veins crystallized; my muscles hardened, going brittle like molten glass cooled too quickly. I fought to keep moving, but my own body had turned against me. The struggle only made me wobble precariously, and the way my body felt I was sure if I hit the ground I'd shatter into a million pieces.

Lucienne Diver

My heart seemed to throw itself against the very walls of my chest, a caged animal frantic for escape. The terror of even my own body out of control had me screaming—but all inside my head, no sound came out. Then that chill stiffness overtook even my thoughts and my mind itself froze.

Chapter Twelve

"You should learn to let sleeping helldogs lie. Don't pull the tail of the cat who swallowed the canary or you will share his fate."

—Pappous in a piece of advice given to Tori while on a bourbon binge

I jolted to awareness as if awaking from one of those falling dreams, only when my body jerked my legs were all that moved. My eyelids barely flickered on command. At first I thought I was still paralyzed from the waist up. Then my teeth started chattering, and I flinched as a wave rode in, momentarily raising the water level to my chin. No wonder I was so cold. I struggled not to panic as I tested my arms and found them to be lashed along with my upper body. Again I tried to open my eyes and this time managed to break through the crust that cemented the lids together. My eyes stung as I opened them, but that didn't seem nearly as immediate as the face of the madman in front of me.

His eyes were still hidden safely behind mirrored glasses, but nonetheless his face managed to convey an intensity, a fervor, reserved for lunatics and zealots. The sight of my own reflection was almost as frightening. I looked like a nixie—

sodden hair dark as night matted to my head, cheeks sunken, lips and lids blue heading toward purple. Clearly I'd received a dunking at some point. It was probably the salt that had crusted then stung my eyes.

I could only pray that Tracy had seen it all from her window and that someone was out looking for me. Surely whatever else she made of the scene it would be clear enough that I'd been carried off. It was a cold comfort, since I could probably rot under the docks until summer before the discovery of my skeleton would ruin some poor tourist's whole day.

"Hey," I said, just to be friendly.

"Tide's coming in," he answered, voice like a boat being dragged over sand.

My lips twisted and I tasted salt. "Gee, thanks for the warning."

"I'm going to watch you die."

"Nothing good on TV tonight, eh?"

He snarled, revealing jagged teeth, too many of which came to a point.

I swallowed and it hurt to get past the constriction in my throat. "So, you're going to drown me like you did Sierra Talbot?" Couldn't hurt to ask. I mean, what was he going to do, kill me? At least maybe I could solve the case before I died.

"Don't try your mind games on me, witch. You know very well I didn't kill Sierra."

"No? Well, you'll pardon me if I'm a bit skeptical, since my lungs are about to fill with that same saltwater."

Another wave came in as if in emphasis, and it was no longer just my lips that were chattering. My whole body had begun to shake, trying desperately to generate its own heat. I wondered how long I had and whether I'd actually have the chance to drown or whether hypothermia would shut me down first.

"What are you talking about," he growled. "She was drained."

Even half-numb and all terrified, I recognized sincere confusion. The scaled menace really believed as I had at first. Which meant there were two killers and I was still going to die with my curiosity less than wholly satisfied.

"Not according to the autopsy. Sierra drowned in her bathtub. *Drowned.* With saltwater in her lungs. Very strange. A locked-room mystery. I'm thinking it had to be one of your ilk."

The snarl was back, along with a second glimpse of all those pointy, shark-like teeth. He lurched forward and grabbed at my hair, nearly tearing it out by the roots. I screeched, straining to move with the pressure, to ease the pain, but it was no good. I scissored my legs, trying to catch his to no avail. His arm was angled so there was no way even to take a bite out of crime.

"You lie!"

I nearly gagged on the scent of rotting fish that wafted over me, but I didn't think now was the time to shill Tic-Tacs.

"Check it out. If I'm wrong, you can kill me later. Something to look forward to. But I'm not wrong."

He stared at me, trying to read the truth, I guessed, all the while upping the abuse to my scalp. I tried not to think about the fact that waves were no longer required for the water level to hit my chin.

"He told me it was Circe." But fish-boy wasn't talking to me. I had a feeling that I'd already ceased to exist for him, which was just as dangerous as being the center of his attention.

"I'm already investigating, so if you would simply—"

"You have already done enough. There are things— No. I will confront him on my own. *You* will die."

The pressure on my scalp vanished and pinpoints of pain stabbed at me.

"But—" I protested.

My captor had vanished along with any hope of reprieve.

I continued to shudder and squirm, lips compressed as the water lapped at them, but whatever he'd bound me with was tougher than I was. I couldn't even hope that somehow one of my forbearers' immortality had been passed to me. Eternity in a watery grave seemed strangely unappealing.

Stretching my neck as long as I possibly could to rise above the water, I risked taking on water to shout and got off two good hollers before choking on a wave.

My vision was starting to do a disturbing fade to black. I strained upward trying to build height where I had none, to raise myself above the surf, but I'd lost feeling in my lower body and could no longer tell if my muscles were responding. My teeth were chattering so hard I nearly bit my tongue, and my brain kept bibbling.

I tried to think, tried so hard to focus on some plan, some object I carried that would help, but my thoughts were like the surf, surging and retreating, impossible to pin down. "*How do you pin a wave upon the sand,*" my brain sang at me. And nuns. Were there *nuns* dancing around in my head? If that didn't signal the end, it certainly should. The four flying nuns of the apocalypse...

Something flickered before me—golden instead of the ominous blue-green of the surf, but I couldn't focus in. It was just an impression.

Next thing I knew everything shifted and I fell forward into oblivion.

I was heartily sick of this oblivion crap. I didn't wake suddenly this time—in fact, I didn't so much wake at all as drift for a while in that semi-dream state where all is cozy contentment. Something niggled at the back of my brain. Somehow all was not as it should be, but I forced the thought away. If the fantasy felt this good, I saw no reason to rush the return of reality. Until I heard the soft snore behind me. The lassitude vanished in the face of a full-frontal adrenaline assault.

I tried to bolt upright, but something heavy anchored me to the bed. And it was a bed. My eyelids had lifted even if nothing else had. *Not again,* I thought.

The room was completely unfamiliar. Beautifully decorated in Mediterranean style, like something out of MTV's *Cribs.* A warming tingle started in the vicinity of my, ah, stomach. I looked down at the arm. Yup, sun-kissed bronze, fine golden hair covering it. The fingers disappeared beneath my ribcage— my very *naked* ribcage!

I squirmed, trying to turn at least, hoping to wake him with the motion. *Uh oh.* Oh, something was awake all right, something long and hard and—I froze. What I really wanted to do was rub myself up against him like a cat, bask in his heat and, now that my senses were up and running, his musky, salty scent. My breathing got ludicrously heavy just thinking about it. But if Apollo were to wake, he'd take it as an invitation and, frankly, not one I'd have the willpower to withdraw.

"Apollo!" I said sharply. Once again I sounded like a rusty gate. I was dimly aware that I should feel that way too, a creaky old gate complaining with every move, but I didn't. Maybe the adrenaline rush was overwhelming my pain receptors. I felt oddly abuzz.

Apollo's fingers flexed against my ribcage, driving all thoughts straight out of my head, especially once he snuggled in, erection unerringly pressing between my butt cheeks. Warm breath stirred my hair, which was nuzzled aside a second later and replaced with lips and then teeth, nipping their way up my shoulder to my neck. The hand holding me swept upward, brushing the underside of my breast.

I said Apollo's name again, but it came out as breathy encouragement rather than rebuke. Then he'd fully palmed my breast, and I found myself pushing back against him, nearly riding his shaft. He moaned.

What was I doing?

Now that his arm no longer pinned me down, I turned.

"Apollo, no."

But his lips closed on mine before I could say more and instead of pushing him away, my hands buried themselves in his ridiculously lush hair. I practically kneaded his head as he rolled me under him and skimmed a hand from breast to hip and back up again to lift my chin so that he could nibble his way down my neck. God, I was already wet and aching. Unable to help myself, I rocked against him, teasing myself against his hard shaft. Mercifully, he'd retained shorts or I would have spread my legs right there and pulled him inside me.

A little part of me tried to reassert sanity. For all I knew his eyes still weren't even open and this was just the continuation of some erotic dream. I raised my head to search out his eyes but all I could see was the crown of his head as he moved down my body. A spike of heat, more liquid than lightning, molten like lava raced through me as his teeth clamped down on one nipple, just on the pleasurable side of pain. I cried out.

He raised his face, finally, to look at me and my heart literally missed a beat. His features hadn't changed and yet there was nothing human in them. He was dangerously, wildly, elementally *powerful*. Gorgeous was too tame and passive a word. His eyes glowed like the sun reflected off the water. I was so overheated I felt I would spontaneously combust.

"Stop," I said.

It was weak, but he did. His whole body stilled, even the rhythm I hadn't realized we'd set. My body throbbed, so close. I couldn't look away from those eyes that still held mine, though I was sure I'd see sunspots into the next century. I couldn't bring myself to say anything more. I didn't want Apollo to take me at my word, but I didn't want to be devoured. There seemed no third option.

"What do you want, Tori?"

I had a lot of answers for that, but none that I wanted to share.

"I can't think when you're on top of me."

He grinned wolfishly.

"That was not supposed to be a compliment," I snapped.

He lowered himself for another kiss, but kept it brief. Even so, it nearly collapsed my resolve. As soon as he moved, I rolled to the side of the bed, taking the sheet with me. Apropos of nothing, I realized they were green with some stylized wave pattern and nearly as soft as a kitten's fur.

"Why am I naked?" I asked, not daring to look at him lest he be doing something terribly provocative, like stroking himself. Whoa. I shoved that mental image straight down into my little black box, possibly to be examined later under very low light.

"I couldn't leave you in your wet clothes. You were soaked through. And before you ask, I laid down next to you to share body heat."

"How did you find me?"

"You're going to interrogate me now?" There was an edge to his voice and a very reckless part of me wanted to make him angry. I wasn't sure if it was to push him away or make him touch me again. Either way, I didn't like it.

"Yes," I said, trying to keep my thoughts out of my voice.

"Police scanner." I heard movement, the slide of fabric, but still couldn't bring myself to look. "I got one when the oracle failed on Circe's death. My assistant monitors it."

All those lovely endorphins were ebbing now and I had the urge to lay myself down on that wonderfully soft bed, but I didn't dare. The strange thing was that I still didn't feel wrung out and shaky as I did after my last bout with the water, just languid. Yet another mystery to ponder. "Okay, so you'd know there'd been a kidnapping. How would you know it was mine or where to find me?"

"No more questions until you answer mine. Tori, look at me." It came out as much plea as command, and it seemed more revealing to refuse than to look him in the eye. "Why won't you let me love you?"

My heart seized, even though I knew he hadn't meant it *that* way, and I told the damned thing to make up its mind. First Armani, now Apollo. I'd never been the fickle type. Damn— *Armani.* We were supposed to have a date tonight. Did he even know what had happened or that I was safe?

"Armani—" I realized as soon as it was out of my mouth that it sounded like an answer to the question—and I wasn't even sure it wasn't. I was so confused.

Apollo's face went hard. "He's a mortal." As if that was an argument.

"Apollo, *I'm* a mortal."

"Not exactly."

"What do you mean 'not exactly'? Either I am or I'm not."

"As you say."

"Don't clam up on me now. You don't get to drop a bomb like that and go all shirty."

"Shirty?"

I bit my lip to keep from screaming and counted to ten. "Let's not start that 'I don't get your newfangled slang' crap. You understand me."

His eyes looked inhuman again, not hot like the sun but cold, like glacial ice. I was an idiot. I'd known what a very bad idea it was to play around with a god. It didn't matter that I'd stopped. I'd given out mixed signals, I'd nearly taken things too far and now I'd hurt his ego if not his feelings.

"Understand *me*," he said, voice thick with power.

The phone rang.

"I will not be ordered about."

It rang again.

"You have refused any claim—"

And again.

"Damn." Apollo stalked to the receiver and swiped it from the cradle. "What?"

The voice coming through was loud enough to be heard at a distance if not understood. Female and all het up about something. I looked around for a bathroom, hoping to find my clothes hung up to dry. I was getting the hell out. If I had to I'd lock myself into my apartment until I got my head on straight or until lack of funds got me booted, whichever came first. I was through with gods, through with men in general and pretty disgusted with myself as well. Not to mention pissed off at my own pity party. Oh yeah, I was in a fine state.

And still naked. As far as I could tell, my clothes had vanished.

It killed any chance of a dramatic exit—or even of slinking out unseen—but I had to go back to Apollo to ask the whereabouts of my clothing.

Apollo didn't react as I reentered the bedroom. He was too busy watching the flat-screen television mounted on the wall. I groaned. Someone had gotten video of the rescue. The news footage exposed Apollo, half-naked, his impressive chest exposed and my flaccid, waterlogged body clutched to it. Apollo looked cinematically heroic. I looked like crap. If the contrast didn't dampen his libido, I didn't know what would.

"Hot damn," he said under his breath.

"Um, my clothes?" I asked uncomfortably from just within the doorway—far enough in that I could see the screen but close enough to a speedy retreat.

"I sent them out," he answered without pulling his eyes away from the screen. "*That* ought to convince the damned studios I'm still leading-man material."

"Huh?"

"I mean, look at Connery. How old was he when he played opposite Zeta-Jones?"

"Right. Before you go staging your comeback, do you think you can find me something to wear so I can get out of your hair?"

146

"I need to call my publicist back. Damn, you can't *pay* for publicity like this. Can't believe she's teed off I didn't tell her first— What did you say?"

My fuse was lit. "Are you saying you rescued me as some freakin' publicity stunt? That's why you wouldn't answer my questions. You probably didn't even know it was me in trouble, just some random damsel in distress."

His face twitched in irritation. "I *did* know it was you, and before you go concocting some crazy conspiracy theory, it's called *scrying*, okay? Damn, you're suspicious. As far as the camera goes, that was just luck—paparazzi, maybe, or some tourist with a handycam."

He rose in all his nekkid glory and headed for a door I'd missed in my avoidance of the bedroom. I tried not to ogle, but really, wow. And I mean *wow*. The big screen did not do him justice. He needed intimate spaces and natural lighting. Oh hell, my hormones were getting all supercharged again.

The sheer vastness of his walk-in closet momentarily distracted me, and I had to fight down the ugly green-eyed monster—jealously, not lust. The blasted thing was the size of my whole apartment.

Apollo's phone was ringing again, but he ignored it from the depths of his closet.

"Do you want me to get that?" I called.

"No. I don't have a damned thing here to give you to wear. I'm going to have to call someone. There are going to be a million questions, and I'll need to coordinate with the police. They'll probably want a press conference."

Phantasmagorical.

"Just give me a T-shirt and some sweats. I'm sure if I roll them they'll stay up long enough to get me home."

Apollo emerged to stare me down. He looked like he was taking calming breaths. "Do you not realize that there are going to be paparazzi everywhere? You can't just walk out the front door. We've got to have a plan, a story. If they recognize you, you'll be shark bait. The fact that I brought you here rather than a hospital will raise questions."

"And heavens forbid you be linked to me."

Tension was rolling off Apollo in waves. "Is that what you want—your fifteen minutes of fame?"

It was too bad Christie and I had such different coloring and I couldn't get her in to be my stunt double. She would eat this up.

"No," I answered.

I knew he was baiting me. He hadn't forgotten my earlier slight or his anger, but for right now he needed me for his impromptu publicity campaign. I wondered if I went along whether I would escape retribution.

"Fine, then I will call Maria. *You* can call Armani. And, by the way, it is quite interesting to me that you use his last name and my first. So, perhaps you think more of me than you realize."

I hated myself for the thrill that sent up my spine. It didn't sound as if Apollo had given up the chase. One would think the first-hand demonstration of what it meant to run with not just a god but an *actor* would have knocked some sense into me. But common sense and my family, if they'd ever been acquainted, had fallen out ages ago.

Still, I was not so far gone I'd agree to perform for a media circus.

Several phone calls, one reaming out from Armani and a *Mission Impossible*-style escape later, I was locked in a car with a repressively silent plainclothes officer in an unmarked sedan heading toward my apartment. Armani and Lau had wanted to be nowhere near Apollo's dog-and-pony show lest the media make the logical leap between the kidnapping and rescue and Circe Holland's high-profile murder case. Some LAPD spokesman had been delegated deflection duty.

I wasn't surprised to see Armani waiting for me when I let myself into my apartment. I didn't ask how he'd gotten in himself. My super was nothing if not mercenary. If the badge hadn't worked, bribery certainly would have done the trick.

Armani sat in the same chair from which he'd interrogated me after my last attack, eyeing me like he was hungry and pissed off about it, which I could relate to. I noted he didn't rush to enfold me in his arms and tell me how relieved he was to see me. Sheesh. When had I gone all girly? *Enfold me in his arms*—gods, I'd gone over to the melodramatic side of the force.

"Hey," I said offhandedly.

The officer had left as soon as he'd seen his replacement. Armani and I now faced off. Or maybe it just seemed like that because I felt guilty, even though there certainly wasn't any ring on my finger and it wasn't like Armani had even declared himself in any way. I mean, I'd had to blackmail him for a date. Here I was with Apollo, powerful, seductive, terrifying, doing his damndest to get me into his bed if not his life and I was still pining over Armani. Maybe it was the *terrifying* part of the aforementioned. Maybe I'd just grown accustomed to Armani's face, but I thought it was more than that. In many ways, Apollo was an amazing, exotic vacation I couldn't really afford and Armani was like coming home.

"Karacis?" *Apollo calls me Tori,* I thought. "You okay? You seem distracted."

Drop it, Tori, there be dragons. I snapped to.

"Fine. Just..." To my horror, tears started leaking from my eyes.

Ridiculously hormonal, teary-eyed, self-reflective. Thank the gods—I wasn't crazy, I was probably just pre-menstrual.

I cackled. Armani halted mid-rise, staring at me like I'd grown a second head.

"Don't worry, I'm not going to fall apart on you." I swiped at the ridiculous tears. "It's only—" my inner imp toyed with the truth, and if I ever wanted him to run screaming, maybe I'd share it. "Never mind. I'm fine now."

He didn't look like he believed me, but he couldn't hover awkwardly over the chair forever, so he finally decided to stand. I took the next move out of his hands by walking right up and putting my arms around him. My head only came to his chest, but it was a really nice chest. He rested his chin on top of my head as he did that sappy enfolding thing. He was warm and comforting. I felt strangely at peace. After a minute, I also realized that we were breathing at the same pace and that his back where my hands gripped it beneath the jacket was just the least bit damp. For some reason, I wanted to explore that.

I drew away before confusion could rear its ugly head again.

"Sit. I'll tell you everything."

He raised an eyebrow. "Everything?" he asked.

I looked at him hard. "What do you mean?"

He shrugged. "You were off the radar for a long time."

Chapter Thirteen

"Just because you have no dreams of glory doesn't mean you get to ruin mine."

"Glory? You're a performer in a rinky-dink, two-bit circus. You can't sacrifice your health for a— Rialto's right behind me, isn't he?"

—last words Tori and her brother shouted at each other before Lenny Rialto blew a gasket and very nearly her family's contract

I laid in bed trying to ignore the figure watching over me like some latter-day gargoyle. Armani was planning to put me under surveillance whether I liked it or not and insisted on taking first shift. I didn't like it, but then I wasn't too fond of fighting for my life either, so a temporary guardian might be the lesser of two evils.

Since he wanted to remain watchful, I doubted Armani would accept an offer of a place to lay his head. He'd gone all quiet when I told him that I'd been unconscious for most of the missing time and even more so somehow when upon further questioning I accounted for Apollo's whereabouts. I left out exactly what had transpired when I awoke, but I had the awful feeling that Armani was filling in his own blanks. I couldn't very well stop him without confessing to what *had* happened, which was bad enough.

I finally fell off to sleep, only to dream of being chased by coyotes who turned into paparazzi and herded me into the center ring at the big top. To escape I climbed to the high-wire act, where my family tossed me from one to the other while I tried not to shriek like a banshee—until my brother's shoulder gave out. Then I plummeted toward certain death.

I awoke sweaty, thrashing and alone. Second watch, I guessed, hadn't been invited in, for which I was grateful. Even though I was sure the surveillance was completely unnecessary, I felt I had to know where my watcher was—just in case. Muscles protested, but only vaguely, as I got up to wash away the sweat with a cool cloth. The bathroom mirror reflected back at me a rumpled, sleepy-eyed image. If this was the vision that had greeted Apollo, it was a wonder we'd gotten to first base. Anyway, even with my nightshirt ending three-quarters of the way down my thigh, I reckoned it safe enough to peer out my doorway to see how close by my babysitter might be. I was unlikely to incite more than a grimace.

I'd wondered if the surveillance would be as far away as a squad car on the street, but no, Armani had opted for aid closer at hand—a baby-faced patrolman whose five a.m. shadow seemed incongruous. He looked up from his paper as my bedroom door opened, raked me with a glance and a nod and went back to his reading. Yup, I was definite siren material.

I drew my head back in, set the deadbolt, unset it again, figuring that with my enemies trouble might not come knocking at the front door; it might not be the best idea to lock out aid. With that happy thought, I resumed the supine position. It was a long, long time before I gave in once more to sleep.

Yiayia was on a roll.

"...clutched to his chest for gods' sake and you don't *call*..."

It had been a good ten minutes since she'd awakened me from a fitful sleep, and I had yet to get out a single word in my own defense.

I cut in finally, "Yiayia, I was a little busy being *passed out*, thank you very much, then being interrogated before passing out again. I promise that I would have called you if only you'd given me the chance to wake up at a decent hour."

There was a weighty silence while Yiayia measured my sins against my suffering.

"Fine, you are forgiven, but only if you tell me everything. How did he feel? Was he sexy as hell?"

"Yiayia!" I gasped in astonishment. "For one thing, I was *unconscious.*"

She clucked her tongue at me. "*Then.* Do not try to tell me that you've had no private moment. It cannot be a coincidence that you start digging into the gods' lives and then Apollo himself rescues you from the deep. You have been holding out on me." She sniffed, "You will get no more from me until you come clean."

Gods, she was getting as bad as me with the slang. Maybe we'd both seen one too many cop shows. Heavens knew I'd get no peace until I complied. Anyway, I needed someone to talk to.

I poured it all out, more or less. Apollo, Armani, my confusion, the case itself, the conclusions we'd come to, everything I knew of my attacker.

She hesitated only an instant once I wound down, as if to be certain that I was done.

"I will not tell you what to do, since you have never listened anyway. Whatever you decide with your men, go carefully.

Apollo...I think you know the dangers already. He may burn you out or leave you still burning with no way for another to ever take his place. But if you should choose your detective, it will not be any safer, certainly not for him. You've heard the stories of scorned gods. Just know I am here for you, whatever you need."

I tabled that, since my only choice was no choice at all. I would not be subsumed by some god, no matter how sexy, and Armani seemed to have taken himself out of the running. Anyway, my love life was the least of my concerns.

Yiayia beat me to a change of subject. "Regarding your attackers, I would say Glaucus, but in all the pictures I've seen of him, he has a tail like a serpent. Of course, it is possible that he has found some potion or spell to allow him to walk like a man once again. It sounds like his Mo—" I thought she meant M.O., as in modus operandi, but she pronounced it like one of the Three Stooges, "—is falling in love with an inappropriate woman like that actress only to have something horrid happen. Just think of that poor Scylla, a monster for all eternity because Circe double-crossed him on that love potion."

It made perfect sense. Glaucus, having been betrayed by Circe in the past, wouldn't have had any trouble believing that she'd killed his new love. The question was, had someone suggested it to him—manipulated him into Circe's murder? And was that the whole purpose of Sierra Talbot's death or was there more?

While Glaucus now sported eternally in the surf, he'd once been a humble fisherman, transformed by some magical mystery herb he'd found on a deserted island. The herb hadn't done a damned thing, though, to ease the transformation or extend his human lifespan. For that he was beholden to the water gods and goddesses, who'd made him a pet project, taken him under their wings and granted him divinity. Whether

Glaucus's initial metamorphosis was unstable or some new monkey wrench had been thrown into the works, it was not out of the realm of possibility that he could regrow legs. Neither was it inconceivable that beings with such long lifespans had memories to match and that someone like Glaucus could still feel such a debt of gratitude that he'd be prone to unquestioning faith in his saviors.

"Your contact?" I asked, dragging my focus back to the conversation. "Has he said anything about what's going on?"

Yiayia sighed heavily. "He has been—evasive, hard to reach. I have half a mind to fly out there myself and demand answers. If we were on hiatus..."

I laughed. "Yiayia, if only you could get out here to kick butt and take names, we'd have this whole mess cleared up in no time."

"Darn straight."

"One more thing—where's Hermes hiding out these days?"

"Do you not know?" She tsked. "This younger generation, they never listen to us molden oldies. He is a syndicated columnist, Thom Foolery."

Strangely enough, Yiayia's call had invigorated me. I'd closed the door on my silly urge-to-give-up pity party and was ready to jump back into things.

Sadly, before I could do anything else, my presence was required down at the station. Lau and Armani, as he'd told me last night, were under increasing pressure to close the Holland and Talbot cases. The chief was maybe twenty-four hours away from ordering a task force. Even knowing it was futile, Armani had passed along the insistence that I come in to work with a police sketch artist. I wondered what the hell I was going to say. I didn't want to forever ruin my credibility by playing unobservant, but neither could I have the unsuspecting populace turning in some poor man who just happened to look like a made-up perp. Of course, I had held right from the beginning that there was something odd about Circe's killer, so it would serve them right if I gave them the Swamp Thing.

Chafing at the senseless waste of time, I grabbed a scone and latte on the way to the station to ease my pain. I even grabbed a large dark roast for my shadow, who had pulled over when I did.

Armani was either out following another lead or on Hephaestus watch, but Lau, just as pleasant as ever, babysat my efforts. She huffed and puffed over the ridiculousness of my description, as if she had no idea what was really going on. I was as impressed as I was irritated at her performance.

After the sketch artist finally threw in the towel, Lau and I had a little one-on-one. The stake-out of Hiero Cholas was off. He'd deserted his little *pied a terre* to return to his home base near San Marino. It might have meant that we were completely wrong about Hiero being one of the co-conspirators—only he'd chosen to rent a truck and load all his worldly goods onto it for the trip. It didn't bode well. If I looked good in sandwich board, I'd be going around with a sign saying "The End is Near". Or, what the hell, "Nigh". Might as well wax poetic before the end. It wasn't as if La La Landians didn't see weird crap every day and would pay me any heed.

With nothing but a crazy story even the SyFy Channel would reject as too "far out", there was no way to convince the San Marino PD to keep tabs on Cholas. There was no way to monitor packages he might send out or avenues back into the city. Lau had, apparently, convinced Cholas's super here in L.A. to let her know if he returned, but the long and short of it was we'd lost him.

I *hated* this part of an investigation, the part where the trails all petered out, where you had to clear-cut a new path without a compass. If this were a dime novel, now would be about the time for a wild hunch. If I were Sherlock Holmes I'd no doubt have made some logical leap that would leave my everyman partner in awe of my deductive reasoning. As it was, I retreated to my car, pulled the notebook I used to keep track of mileage from above my visor and nibbled on the end of the accompanying pencil while I took refuge in a loose-ends list. I liked lists—they made you feel like you were doing something even when you weren't. Plus, it felt so good to cross things off.

1- Find out whether Christie knew Circe

(Yeah, I was reaching, but I never had gotten an answer and that niggled at me.)

2- Find Hermes

3- Find Mrs. S's damned dog

4- Figure out what the hell Apollo meant when he said I was "not quite" mortal

5- Why wasn't I weak and jittery from my second water escape?

6- Explosives: where from, where set?

7- Which old ones have been jittery or disappearing?

(It was something Apollo had mentioned in passing and a question I should have asked earlier.)

7- Yiayia's mystery man?

I probably could have gone on all day avoiding real work by coughing up questions, but the thought of me and the rest of L.A. at the bottom of the ocean was pretty damned motivating. Somehow I sensed that Cholas's move had started the countdown. Maybe it was Apollo's gift of precognition, maybe it was just those investigator's instincts I was supposed to have belatedly kicking in. Either way we were screwed.

It irritated the hell out of me that before I could even get to my list I had one very important errand to run—replacing the cell phone Glaucus or whoever had dunked in our very first ocean encounter. I felt oddly cut off from the world without it and certainly from the all-important 9-1-1 in case of emergency, which the way my life was going was not a question of whether but of when. So, with a semi-quick stop at the Radio Shack I'd passed on the way to the station, I rejoined the twenty-first century.

No sooner had the door hit my fanny on the way out than the phone rang. I checked the readout. Jesus.

"Yes?" I answered.

"Boss lady, I mean no disrespect, but where the hell are you?"

I blinked.

"The phone has been ringing off the hook. Apollo actually sounds *desperate*—"

Two beeps cut across Jesus's rant.

"You gave him my cell number," I accused.

"I'm surprised you didn't. I mean, aside from the fact that *E Magazine* named him last year's sexiest man alive—"

My jaw ached from clenching. "I'll take this up with you later," I threatened, jamming my finger on the button to cut him off and send Apollo through. At least my virtue was safe over the phone. In theory.

"Karacis Investigations," I answered, as if I hadn't recognized the number.

"Tori, you have to come forward," Apollo demanded without preamble.

"'Scusé?"

"Without a grateful victim, there are some rumors that the rescue was a publicity stunt. I need you in front of a camera."

Sure, ten million or so registered SAG actresses would give their eyeteeth for such an opportunity and *I* got the call.

"No."

"Tori—" He imbued it with a boatload of mojo. Even sitting my knees went weak.

"Still no. Hire someone."

"I've hired you."

"For an investigation. Not to put my life under a magnifying glass."

He muttered something under his breath. "If I hire some actress, it's bound to come out, and then my name will be mud. All because I saved your life. I didn't want to play this card, but *you owe me.*"

There they were, those dreadful words. I hadn't asked for any of this and still the bill had come due. I just hadn't expected it so soon.

"The whole life-debt thing, eh? Look, I'd be glad to give my life literally. Any time you want me to leap in front of a bullet or save you from a watery grave, just say the word. Promise. But that's a one-time deal. If I do this, I'm going to keep paying. Your damned press will pry into my background, lurk outside my door—" talk to my family, "—and make it impossible to do my job. You know, the one you hired me to do?"

He was momentarily hushed. "I don't suppose you have a sister?"

That surprised a laugh out of me. "Brother. And let me tell you, there's not enough hot wax in the world to pass him off as a woman."

"Pity."

I waited. It couldn't be that easy.

"Someday—" Apollo's voice dropped low, gravelly, to a dead-on impression of The Godfather, "—and that day may never come—I'll call upon you to do a service for me."

"Cute," I said wryly.

"I was going for clever."

"Be glad I gave you cute."

"You are possibly the most contrary woman I've ever met."

"Am not."

"I know what you're doing."

"Rolling my eyes?"

"*Argotera*, Tori."

"Anh anh ah—not so fast. I want some answers first. What's this about my mortality?"

"Tori, my battery's dying. I have to go." And just like that he was gone.

I was steamed. This time not in the good way. There'd been no telltale sound or lack thereof, on my end anyway, signaling a foundering battery. That meant evasion; he was hiding something. Finding out what meant more contact than was probably healthy.

It hit me in a flash that my own curiosity was truly the only thing connecting us now. I'd solved the case Apollo had hired me to investigate. I might not be able to prove to a court of law that Poseidon had drowned Sierra Talbot and implicated Circe, leading to her murder, but conviction wasn't my job. I didn't know whether to be offended or relieved that Poseidon hadn't seen me as enough of a threat to drown. Maybe he thought Glaucus would take care of that as well. Anyway, as soon as I turned in a report, my association with Apollo would come to an end. A mischievous thought flitted past, that I could withhold my information as a bargaining chip for the answers *I* wanted, but I was too professional to do it. I put temptation behind me and headed for the office.

If Jesus had possessed a smidgeon of sense, he'd have run for the hills as soon as he saw the whites of my eyes. Instead, he sat behind his desk as though it was an executive model made of pure mahogany rather than veneer over pressboard and actually had the nerve to put *me* on hold with a raised finger while he continued his telephone conversation.

Only the tightest rein on my fury and the fact that it seemed to involve Mrs. Strohmeyer's missing hound kept me from disconnecting on his behalf.

When he finally hung up, I took a deep breath, ready to lay into him with a stream of words and run-on sentences, but Jesus beat me to it.

"Look, *chica*, I do not appreciate being thrown into the middle of your lover's quarrels," he said, looking for all the world like a pissy librarian glaring through *pince-nez* even thought he'd never be caught dead in the damned things.

"What the hell?" I burst.

"Apollo-freakin'-Demas, *sí?* I don't know what you do to get a man so worked up but honest to god, *chica*, you are going to share the secret or I will key your personal information into every Internet dating scheme I find."

I shuddered. "Jesus, I promise that when all this is over I will take you out for one helluva thank-you dinner and tell all."

I hoped he didn't notice my crossed fingers. "For now, can we get back to work?"

He eyed me like a Rodeo Drive sales girl. "One thing first, I must know, stud or dud?"

I groaned.

Chapter Fourteen

"If you assume you know nothing, you're going to be right a good part of the time."

—*Uncle Christos, in a huh? moment when discussing how to begin an investigation without preconceptions*

Even with time ticking away on the potential plot to remodel the California coastline, I couldn't ignore the message leading possibly to Mrs. S's hound. We'd finally gotten a hit on one of the "Lost Dog" posters. I didn't think it was any coincidence that it hadn't happened until Mrs. S had okayed a reward.

So, I set Jesus the task of locating Thom Foolery, grabbed my supplies and set off after the hound of the Baskervilles. I half felt it should be a dark and stormy night, but it was neither. It was a typical gorgeous L.A. day. You might think that all that sunshine would get monotonous; you'd be wrong.

My brain worked in strange and mysterious ways, especially when I needed a plan to capture the damned hound should the "nice doggie" approach fail. When Mrs. S had first signed on the dotted line, I'd asked her for a few things I thought would help, like a favorite chew toy or blanket that might be used to lure Honey into her carrier. What she'd brought was an old sweatshirt that smelled like its name. It had seemed odd to me at the time, the brand new carrier and the fact that the odiferous shirt, which she said Honey had appropriated, wasn't covered in dog hair. I'd asked whether the dog was a beagle mix, the kind that didn't shed, but she'd just looked at me funny and sworn that Honey was pure hound.

Added to the new information I'd received from Christos's police contacts about the girlfriend, who'd raised a hue and a cry the same week Mrs. Strohmeyer had hired me... Well, I wasn't sure what it meant, but it didn't add up, at least not to a nice round number.

My job was limited to finding the elusive hound. Period. I had more than enough trouble already without looking for more. Really. Still, it was a mystery and I'd swear to bloodhound rather than gorgon in my own background based on that part of me baying in protest at the thought of giving up the hunt.

I was headed toward East Hollywood, not too far from the Sunset Strip where I'd first heard the hound baying. Interestingly enough, the address of our tipster and that of Dick Strohmeyer's girlfriend were the same—same building anyway. I wondered whether dog and master had been shacked up with the mistress—and if so why she'd cried bloody murder—or if the hound had followed a scent trail to his owner. I tried to tell myself to mind my own business and stick to the matter at hand, but that had never worked.

Anyway, on arrival Jane Kleinschmidt was waiting for me outside the entrance to an apartment complex like any other. The lady herself could have come from central casting—that indeterminate age between middle and old, housedress, sweater, sensible slipper-shoes. She scanned the walkway, presumably looking for me, though she passed me over when I came into range, only to snap back a moment later as the cage I carried registered.

"Oh, you're— Somehow, I thought you'd be bigger, you know, more *butch.*"

Ooo-kay.

My lack of response seemed to unsettle her. "Anyway, ah, hello. I'm Jane Kleinschmidt, but I guess you know that if you're here."

"Yes, ma'am. You reported a hound?"

"Lord yes. I'd gone down to get my laundry and there he was, followed me into the stairwell. He's still there unless someone let him out. I certainly didn't. I would have called Animal Control, but I'd seen your posters and taken the number. Just in case, you know, since there's reward money and all."

That last sentence was a prompt if I'd ever heard one. I assured her that once the dog's identity was verified, she'd get her reward.

"Oh good. This way."

The lobby of the place wasn't much to look at beyond the mosaic floor. Walls that I'd kindly call taupe made the space darker and closer than it had to be. A few well-placed wall sconces would really—aw hell, Jesus was rubbing off. A heavy door to the right of the elevators let us in to the stairwell, imaginatively painted in stark white with industrial grey railings. It was dead silent.

"What floor was he on when you last saw him?" I asked.

"He followed me as far as the third and then sat whimpering at the doorway. I didn't let him out."

Jeez, I'd take the elevator for two floors let alone more. Mrs. Kleinschmidt was one tough old bird.

"Honey?" I called experimentally.

A tentative woof answered.

"Honey," I called again, feeling completely stupid. I'd thought before that the hound must have been the husband's, but I rethought that now. With a name like Honey, it had to be Mrs. S's damn dog.

This time the response was skittering feet, the sound of dog coming on fast—enthusiastic, I hoped, rather than aggressive. And *finally* I made the acquaintance of the long-lost hound, who stopped on the landing just above to regard me mournfully, wrinkles upon wrinkles, sagging jowls and big soulful eyes. Okay, conceivably cute in a homely sort of way.

"Come here, boy." He cocked his head and I swear gave me the once-over. When his eyes hit the cage he let out such a racket that I immediately held it behind me for Mrs. K to take. She missed the cue entirely, so I shook the carrier. "A little help here?"

Finally, the weight of the carrier was taken from me. I hadn't shifted my eyes off Honey, and he hadn't taken his off me, though he had backed up until his rump hit the wall.

"Okay, Honey, no cage," I soothed. "But your mommy wants you back. Don't you want to go home? Hmm? Nice, warm, all the dog biscuits you can eat." I didn't mention the bath, even though eau de dumpster was starting to drift my way. Wherever Honey had been hanging out, it hadn't been with his owner.

Honey snorted, an inelegant move that involved actual—ew. Anyway, he seemed less than enchanted with the idea of going home.

"What about steak? You like steak, right? I'm sure your mommy will be so glad to have you back, she'll cook you up a nice rare T-bone."

He whimpered and allowed me to take two steps forward before he bolted back up the steps. I cursed and raced after him, only to stop short at the third-floor landing where he waited, looking from me to the fire door and back to me. Okay, so we were playing doggie charades.

"You want to see your daddy?" I asked, feeling dumber by the second. "I'll tell you what—you let me get this leash on you and I'll take you to see him." Right, like he could understand me. Still, he cocked his head consideringly. I could hear Mrs. K making her way up the stairs toward us. Fearing her appearance would make the dog bolt again, I tried to hold him on eye contact alone.

"Come on, Honey."

To my amazement, he started toward me, slowly, not fully committed. I held out one hand for him to sniff, though I wasn't sure his olfactory sense was still intact after the garbage he had to have wallowed in. My other hand prepared the leash. Once he'd sniffed and even given my hand a tentative lick, I held the leash out for him to see. He gave it a sidelong glance but otherwise ignored the move.

"Is it him?" Mrs. K asked behind me.

Honey and I both turned to give her a look.

"I think so. I'll need to confirm," I answered evenly, reaching into my pocket for two of my cards. "One of these is for you to keep. The other is for you to write down your information, including social security number so that I can send your check."

"My social?" she asked suspiciously.

"One thousand dollars. Yup, you're going to have to claim it for taxes."

"Damn." It sounded wrong coming out of little Mrs. K.

While she set the carrier down and frisked herself for a pencil, I focused back on Honey, who almost looked to be smiling. At least his wrinkles didn't seem to sag quite so much.

I'd have smiled in return if the cilia in my nose hadn't been singed off by his scent. Instead, wrinkling my own nose, I reached for Honey. I cringed as I walked my fingers through his muck-stiffened fur to find a collar to hook the leash onto. But there was none.

The little lightbulb in my head finally flared. If I hadn't been in the midst of so much weirdness lately, I never would have considered it. Which led me to wonder how many other things I'd missed in my ignorance.

Honey sat patiently now that he'd gotten his point across by pantomime, so I looped the leash around his neck and hooked it back on itself in lieu of a collar.

"Here's my info," Mrs. K cut in. "How do I know I'll get my money?"

"Mrs. Kleinschmidt, you've got my information. You already know the number you have is good because you reached me there. If I'm not straight with you, report me to the Better Business Bureau."

"Don't think I won't. Cage thingy's on the landing." She humphed off up the staircase, muttering under her breath about having to sanitize the building after that filthy dog.

"Well, *Honey*," I said, "why don't we go talk with your lady friend?"

Strictly speaking, it wasn't necessary, of course. I had the dog bound now, but I wanted to be really certain of my hypothesis before I confronted Mrs. Strohmeyer. Besides, there was that whole curiosity thing. Not to mention I was reluctant to load that smell into my car.

So, I walked the dog, right through the fire door and up to apartment 3G.

Marla Kelly answered on the second knock, dressed in a sweat suit much like mine the day of Circe's murder, only her stripes were lime green. Her bottle-red hair flared artistically around her face.

The first words out of her mouth were, "Lord, what is that stench?"

I looked down at Honey, who was wagging his tail furiously and pulling at the leash, eager to brush up against Marla.

"Ew! Get your damned dog away from me."

"Honey, heel," I ordered.

Instead, he lurched again, brought up short when the leash became a noose. Marla cringed back, making ready to slam the door in our faces.

"Wait!" I cried, "I'm here about Dick Strohmeyer."

She froze, even though Honey was now sniffing at a very delicate area.

"May we come in?"

"Fuck no." She swatted at Honey. "Your dog needs to be hosed down. What about that son-of-a-bitch?"

I understood what Santos and Robbins had said about her mouth.

"You mean the *Strohmeyers'* dog, right? Honey?"

Marla shuddered. "Not on your life. If Dick had a dog I never would have set foot in that house. Is this some kind of joke? Did his wife send you? You tell her I haven't seen the fucker in, like, a week and a half. So, if he's run off it's with some other bitch. But—" she leaned in from the waist, trying to keep the rest out of Honey's range, "—I think she offed him. He wouldn't have run out on *me*, I can tell you."

She hadn't sounded so sure of that a moment ago, but I didn't think it would do me any good to point it out.

Marla stared at me in challenge a beat longer before asking. "Is there anything else?"

I shook my head no and the door slammed shut before I could bring it back center.

"Wow, you sure can pick 'em, *Dick*."

I didn't have time for this. I had bigger fish to fry. Not to mention, accusing your client of husband transmogrification was probably not the best way to assure payment. But though I'd already decided that Dick was appropriately named, I just couldn't leave him as he was. Based on scent alone, I guessed he sucked at being a dog.

Before I let Dick into the car, I popped the trunk and exchanged the dog carrier for the emergency blanket I kept back there and spread it over as much of the backseat as I could cover. I also rolled down the windows. When I finally let him inside, I told him to stay, threatening him with a bill for brand-new seats when he was back in man form if any smell or stain lingered. I was tempted to use the gorgon mojo to enforce it, but I didn't need the world to know of the power and didn't trust Dick as far as I could throw him.

The drive from East Hollywood to West was the longest of my life. I'd swear we hit every light. I'd called Mrs. S while stopped at one of those lights to assure that she'd be home. My eyes were watering by the time we pulled up in front of her building.

My phone went off just as I pulled up into her lot. Honey started baying, and I told him in no uncertain terms to shut it or get used to having his butt sniffed. He clammed up, but eyed me like he'd pee on my shoes at the first opportunity.

I checked the readout on the phone: Jesus.

"Watcha got?" I asked.

"Only all the personal data on Thom Foolery. Wasn't easy, let me tell you. All he gives on his website is a Hotmail address and a P.O. Box. Luckily, I have this hacker friend—"

"Stop. What I don't know I can't testify to in court."

Jesus sniffed. I knew I was going to pay for not acknowledging his genius. Last time I'd ticked him off, he'd number-coded the copier so that I couldn't use it without going through him until I figured out his combination.

"Jesus, it's not that I don't appreciate it, because I do. You're absolutely fantastic to put yourself out like that."

"Too little, too late, *chica*. I think a bonus must be involved."

Well, in theory, as soon as I submitted my report and bill to Apollo, I'd have some money to burn. That was, if we weren't all dropped into the drink, in which case the point was moot.

"Fine. When all this is over, you've earned yourself a bonus."

He was awfully quiet.

"Jesus?"

"You ruin all my fun. Now how do I lord this over you?"

I cursed colorfully in Greek. *Men.*

"I'm hanging up now," I told him. "When I do, would you pretty please with sugar on top leave a message with all the information on my voice mail. I'll let it ring through."

Jesus sighed dramatically. "On the condition that you either teach me to swear in Greek or curse me out in English so that I know when it's time to swear blood vengeance."

I couldn't help but laugh at the mental picture of Jesus all dressed up—or rather, barely dressed—as Rambo. He rang off in a huff.

"Well, Dick, shall we face down Mrs. S?"

He gave a soft woof and no resistance as I got him out of the car. The gentleman who held the outer door open for us nearly gagged as we slid past, Dick all the while trying to sniff him and me too preoccupied manipulating the carrier through the entry to keep the canine at bay. I smiled in apology.

When I rang the bell for the Strohmeyers' condo, Mrs. S buzzed us up without even asking who we were.

She stood in the doorway as we approached, eyes only for the hound. The bad streak job in her hair seemed to have mellowed out. Her feet were bare. While she wore a button-down shirt, it was untucked over jeans. I guessed it was as casual as she ever got.

"Honey, you're home," she said quietly. Then, as we got right up to her, she added, "Couldn't you at least have cleaned him up first?"

"Not in my job description. Can we come in?"

Dick looked up at her balefully as she took the leash from me. I half expected him to go for her throat, but he must have been smart enough to realize that it wouldn't convince her to undo her handiwork. He tugged and growled as she led him away, probably to be locked up in the bathroom.

Mrs. S winced as she came back down the hallway, followed by the sound of claws scratching at and likely ravaging her bathroom door. She indicated that I should sit, apparently determined to ignore the sound.

"Thank you," she began. "I've—I've really missed that dog."

I looked her dead in the eye. "Mrs. Strohmeyer, I know all about *Honey*. Now, I'm going to watch you write out checks to Karacis Investigations and to Jane Kleinschmidt, who earned the reward money. Then I'm going to give you twenty-four hours before I call the police to tell them the prodigal husband has come home. You've got until then to return him to normal."

She stared at me like I had three heads.

"I don't—I don't know what you're talking about. You're nuts."

We kept up our staring contest until she finally blinked. "Fine, I'll get my checkbook. I do owe you for the return of my dog."

Uh huh. "And the checks *will* clear—are we understood?"

She spared a moment from digging through the purse on her kitchen counter to look daggers at me. "They'll clear."

"Good." I waited for her to tear the checks out before rising to study and tuck them away.

It was probably too late to end our business on a cheerful note. I doubt Karacis Investigations would be receiving any referrals from Mrs. S.

Still. "Mrs. Strohmeyer—" she met my eyes reluctantly, "—divvying up community property is less expensive than a murder conviction."

"Without a body?" she scoffed.

"It's been done before." She seemed to think about that. In any case, I'd done what I could to see that Dick would regain his natural form and live through the experience.

Chapter Fifteen

"Death comes in threes; disaster comes in waves."
—Uncle Christos

Even as odd as this case had been, I felt the buzz of satisfaction that came with a mystery solved. I was feeling pretty good—right up until the time I checked my messages. The first was from Jesus, as expected, the second from Armani.

"Tori, your attacker has been found, unfortunately dead, washed up under the Santa Monica Pier. It's outside our jurisdiction, but Lau and I were called in because of the description. I have no idea what the press will do with this, but I think your gods might be outed a little sooner than intended. There's no way to keep a lid on it. Body's off to the ME now. We're going to need you to ID him as the suspect. Let's just hope this doesn't move up the conspiracy's time table."

Nothing like the threat of impending doom to kill a buzz. I quickly rang Armani back, but got bumped straight to voice mail. I wondered if I'd catch holy hell if I told Apollo about this latest development. Then it occurred to me that he might already know. What if he'd truly recognized my description of Circe's killer and taken matters into his own hands? I couldn't imagine it, but then, I didn't want to. No, my instincts couldn't be trusted on this. I'd have a better sense of the truth if I could tell him face-to-face and see his reaction, though with an actor... Aw hell, it wasn't my place anyway. I was sure Armani would want to do the honors.

The phone rang in my hand—Armani with the address in Santa Monica. The police there were cooperating only so much; the body stayed on their turf, since *this* murder had taken place within their boundaries. If I had to guess, they might also be thinking of the notoriety the body's sheer oddity would bring.

I got there as fast as I could, signed in, showed my ID and the whole nine yards before I was allowed into a stark tiled hallway where I found Armani and Lau stewing in a small waiting area with hazmat-orange couches. I could almost see the steam streaming from Lau's ears.

"Good," she said, and I knew she didn't mean me, "now maybe they'll let us in."

Armani rose to take my arm and lead me across the hall to a set of double doors he rapped on twice. Lau trailed behind.

A man whose hair had all fled to his monobrow and mustache opened one side far enough to glower at us.

"She's here," Armani said simply.

"I'll take it from here," Monobrow answered.

"Our witness, our escort."

I felt like the rag in a game of tug-of-war.

"Boys, can we play 'mine's-bigger-than-yours' later? I'd like to get this over with." I tightened my grip on Armani's arm to make it clear he'd be coming with.

"Fine," Monobrow said with poor grace, "but don't touch anything, and I don't want a whiff of this hitting the press before we're ready to make a statement. One word and I won't look any further for the leak. Clear?"

I wondered if he was married. He and Marla Kelly would make a lovely couple.

The thought made me smirk. "Yes, your surliness."

He gave me the eye, but after facing down psychos and gods, I couldn't really be impressed. "I don't like your attitude," he growled.

"No problem. I don't like yours."

He didn't have any choice about letting us in, not if he wanted some semblance of an ID, but he didn't have to like it.

Besides the still body on the gurney, there were two other people in the room, one a Junoesque African-American woman in a lab coat, hair pulled into a neat bun, and the other the somewhat-less-chiseled version of A. Martinez. If I weren't already juggling attractions to Armani and Apollo, my hormones might have done a little, "Hey, sailor."

In contrast to his partner, Detective Rodriguez, as he was introduced, gave us a grim smile.

Dr. Sheridan had barely looked up from the body as she continued her discussion already in progress.

"This is too important to treat lightly," she argued with the detective.

"As I've said, the department just doesn't have the resources to cover an unnecessary procedure. Do you know what an MRI costs? Unless you need it to determine cause of death..."

"It might be unimportant to the law, but its value to science—"

"Then let some science foundation pay for it once the body's released," Rodriguez cut in.

Dr. Sheridan looked thunderous, but also seemed to note finally that they had an audience. Still, she offered one final argument. "Once I cut into him, the body won't be intact; so much of the value is lost."

"Enough," Monobrow—Detective Mikulski—cut in. "Argue on your own time or take it up with the chief. Ms. Karacis would like to take a look at our vic."

Rodriguez and Sheridan both eyed me as if to see if I could stand the shock. Then Dr. Sheridan peeled back the sheet, releasing the incongruous smell of ocean salt and singed flesh.

It was fish-face all right. He certainly hadn't gone gently into that good night. His face was a mask of anger. I could just barely see the top of a blackened chest wound. Without a better look, I had no idea if the cause of death was man-made, like a large caliber bullet from a gun held at close range, or godly, like a lightning bolt. So I asked.

"How did he die?"

"Is that the man you saw kill Circe Holland?" Mikulski asked.

"Yes. I believe he may have been stalking Sierra Talbot as well."

It implied that Glaucus had killed both, but it was for the best. He was too dead to care about his reputation and I suspected that Poseidon, if Sierra was indeed his handiwork, was a bit beyond human justice. Anyone looking for him would probably land on a matching slab. Better to put the whole thing to rest.

Mikulski nodded and Dr. Sheridan replaced the sheet.

"You didn't answer my question," I reminded him.

"No, and I'm not going to. For one thing, the autopsy results aren't in. For another, it's none of your damned business."

I was escorted out. Lau reminded him before the door shut on us that they'd be in touch.

"What's his deal?" I asked.

"He's on the wagon," Lau answered. "Happens every time. Weirdly, he's much more charming when he backslides."

Armani gave her an odd look.

"We have history."

I had the office all to myself. Armani and Lau were on duty; Jesus had gone home or wherever he went when he left here. There was no one to hear me scream or cry or rant like a lunatic. I wanted to do it all at once. I didn't like feeling powerless, a teeny tiny ant compared to the huge, unapproachable power of the gods. It made me angry and the anger felt huge, too big for me to contain—as if all hell were literally about to break loose. It gave me the brass balls I needed to threaten a god.

I punched in the number Jesus had found for Hermes in his Thom Foolery persona. When his machine picked up I started talking. "Hermes, I know it's you. Glaucus is dead. You'd better damn well pick up. If I have to fly to Boca to kick your   sorry ass—"

"Please, tell me more," he purred into the phone. "I just love it when women talk dirty to me."

"That was *not* foreplay."

"Not to you, maybe. Really, tracking a man down might be considered forward by some, but I like a little aggression in my women. Of course, now you've blown my whole mystique."

"Whatever. Look, I need to know everything you know. I don't have time for riddles. Three people are dead already—"

"And that's supposed to make me talk? I'm not foolish enough to set myself up as the next victim."

"Then try this on for size—either you tell me and I keep it to myself that you're my source, or I find out elsewhere and put it out that the information came from you."

"It occurs to me that if you 'put it out' that you know, you're in as much danger as me. Maybe more. I've had centuries to prepare for anything."

"Well, damn. That always works on TV."

He chose not to comment.

"Then how about this, I keep completely silent and no one knows the beans have been spilled."

"Until you swoop in to foil the plans. Anyway, I'm not certain I'm so enamored of my current reality that I wouldn't welcome a change."

"Exactly when did you get that stick implanted up your butt? Where's the Puckish rabble-rousing? Come on, you're not really going to hang back and let things unfold without your interference. What fun would that be?"

He laughed. "A very palpable hit. Let me think. How can I keep you in the game without exposing myself? You've caught me at a loss. All that disingenuous idiocy is not without cost, you know."

Hermes made thinking noises until I was ready to jump through the phone line and throttle the answers out of him. Just as my very last nerve was about to snap, he said, "I've got nothing. I only hope you don't unearth the plot too late."

He was gone. My stomach sank down to my toes.

Struggling not to lose hope, I pulled out my list. I wondered if Jesus's hacker buddy could get access to Yiayia's phone records, track down her "friend". I wasn't ready to cut off the very last tie to my family now that Uncle Christos had fled into the wild blue yonder. Not yet anyway. Both Apollo and Hermes had dodged my questions.

Maybe I should have started with Christie and worked my way up. I owed her a call anyway. Aside from emailing her Jesus's head-shot preferences, I'd been ducking her since slipping out of the nightclub with Apollo. She'd want details. Girlfriends told each other that kind of thing, I knew. It was just kinda hard to get used to. In the circus everyone knew each others' business; there was hardly a need to talk about it. Anything truly private was guarded like Fort Knox. The only way to survive in such close quarters day in and day out was to respect that. My fatal flaw. I was good at blowing things wide open. Not so good at sharing.

I sucked it up and dialed Christie's number.

"Hey, traitor," she answered.

"Um, hey?"

"Don't say it like you're not sure I'm talking about you. You practically disappeared off the face of the earth."

"I know. I'm sorry. A lot's been going on."

"Yeah, I saw the news. Looks like you and Apollo are getting pretty chummy. Are you ditching me for a guy? I mean, at least I can sort of understand this one, but—"

"Christie, I'm not ditching you for Apollo or anyone else. It's this case. Well, two really, but I just wrapped up the one."

"Well, goody for you," but the vehemence was already draining from her voice and for once I really appreciated the bigness of heart that allowed Jack the jerk so many chances.

"Actually, maybe you can help me with the other."

"Really?" She brightened.

I grimaced, certain she had something other than interrogation in mind. "Yup. On the day of Circe's murder, the conversation kind of took a right turn before you got to tell me whether or not you knew her."

"Oh."

Noncommittal, but, hey, not outright hostile.

"Do you?" I pushed.

Silence.

"Christie, I can't hear your head shaking."

"Well, duh. I was just trying to decide what to say. See, you're going to think I'm nuts."

"I promise, whatever you have to say, I won't think you're nuts. I've seen enough insanity these last few days that it's starting to seem normal."

"Okay," she answered doubtfully. "Um, here goes—Circe Holland contacted me, like, a year ago about representation."

"She's your agent?" No, that couldn't be right. I was sure she called him something like Mac.

"No, that's the crazy thing. You're going to think I'm all superstitious, but it seems like she's kind of a Typhoid Mary. Her actors are all, like, big, you know, for a short time, kind of shooting stars, but there's no staying power—they die young or fade away. Maybe it's just that her attention wanders to the next big thing. Maybe it's the nature of the business. I just get this weird vibe. But, you know, *Circe Holland*. So, I met with her, took a look at her contract. I can't remember now, but there was something strange about it." Yeah, like a forget spell, I thought. A clause like that doesn't just slip your mind. "Anyway, I didn't sign. Look how well that's turned out—still doing commercials and catalogue shoots."

"Oh, Christie, you did the right thing. *Trust* me."

I'd been ridiculously arrogant thinking Christie needed me to be some kind of guardian angel shielding her from the world. Maybe she already had a guardian angel. Recent events had proven there were more things on Earth than were thought of in my philosophy. Anyway, she did just fine. Probably better than I would have if someone offered up my dreams on a silver platter.

"Really? I'm not a silly superstitious freak? I know you think I'm naïve—"

Ouch. "No, you're just right. I'm the idiot. I'm such a cynic I think it's the only way to be." I needed to start giving Christie more credit. "I'm sorry."

"Good. That way you'll be beholden to me, which works out because, ah, I wanted to ask you something. Just to see what you think. You can always say no, or—"

"Christie, just ask."

"Okay, well, like, I heard that Apollo is taking over Circe's business—hey, wait, that's weird, they're both totally Greek names, right? Anyway, I was wondering if you thought he might consider me again, you know, if he were changing that contract boilerplate, and hoped you could put in a good word?"

I didn't groan, but it was a close thing. I didn't want to owe any more to Apollo than he already thought I did. But for Christie...

"I'll have to play it by ear. He's—" how to put this? "—not always so approachable."

"Uh huh. He looked pretty approachable the other night at the Kasbah," she teased.

I let my head fall until it thumped on my desk. "Ow."

"Tori?"

After the call I sat staring at my blotter for a full minute. Something about the conversation had sparked the glimmer of a thought, but it remained stubbornly out of reach. I was pretty disgusted with myself for taking things for granted. Weeks ago, I *knew* that Yiayia was eccentric and our family stories a bunch of hooey; gods didn't roam the earth, magic existed only in books and movies; blond plus big-hearted equaled dupe. Blind, deaf and dumb. Some investigator.

That was when it hit me, the niggling thought. Since when had Hermes ever been at a loss for words? I had assumed that he was on the level when he told me "I got nothing", but Hermes/Coyote was never that straightforward. I was on the tail end of a planet-sized learning curve about assumptions. What kind of idiot would count her change at any deli but take a trickster god at his word? My kind of idiot, apparently. Uncle Christos was going to regret leaving me alone with his business.

But dammit, I was going to see this through. I thought back over Hermes's parting words. "I hope you don't unearth the plot"—was that it? I didn't see what I could do with the first part, so I moved on to "unearth". I grabbed a piece of blank paper from my printer and started writing. *Unearth—excavate, exhume, dig up, uncover.* Hmmm. *Plot—of land, grave, plan.* Exhume and grave would go together, but if so, whose grave? Hell, for all I knew this could be the plot of a novel or screenplay. It could mean anything. Was I making erroneous assumptions again, trying to read into Hermes's words? Maybe. But I figured it couldn't hurt to put it on my backbrain, see what developed, whereas ignoring the possibility might be hazardous to L.A.'s health.

My stomach growled and the phone rang all at once. I ignored the one and answered the other.

Without preamble, Armani asked, "Are you near a TV?"

"No."

"You might want to find one. I've got some things to wrap up. Then, if it's all right, I'll come by. I'll bring dinner."

Much as I hated to nix what sounded like Armani's attempt to make good on that date... "I'm headed out for something now. You could bring dessert."

"What do you like?"

"Anything chocolate."

I stopped for takeout souvlaki and ate it in front of my television. I flipped through the channels until I found what Armani wanted me to see—the press conference already in progress.

Detective Rodriguez and a man I didn't recognize, but major brass, a captain by his bars, shared the mic while Monobrow tried not to sulk too obviously about his strictly supporting role. Someone must have decided that Rodriguez would make a better impression in front of the cameras. Go figure.

From the sea of raised hands, brass chose a brunette Barbie in a red power suit.

"We've heard that there are some unusual identifying characteristics about the body that was fished out of the ocean. Would you comment on that?" Which either meant a leak or, more likely, that whoever found the body had already contacted the stations about selling camera-phone pictures or amateur video to the highest bidder.

Brass oh-so-kindly sidestepped that one, leaving Rodriguez with the mic. "Yes, our victim has certain abnormalities, as noted by one of the witnesses at the Circe Holland homicide, a local investigator."

Reporters clamored for attention, shouting questions about my identity, the nature of the abnormalities. Somebody brought up the *X-Files.*

I leaned forward, realizing only when I ran out of air that I was holding my breath.

Brass stepped in then, "Okay, ladies and gentlemen. That's all we have for you right now. The investigation is still ongoing."

Oh Lord of the Rings, the cat was out of the bag now. I could think of only one reason the gods would allow Glaucus's body to be found. They were ready to make themselves known. We were out of time.

I turned off the television in favor of my laptop. Every single hourglass was a saw-stroke to my nerves. Even cable was too slow.

There were roughly a bazillion government and academic websites dealing with the San Andreas fault system, none of which were overlaid by city or county maps so that I could see if any fissures ran beneath a cemetery or any other sort of plot. By flipping back and forth between a fault diagram and a map of the San Fernando Valley, I was able to get a very general sense of locations, but that was it.

After an hour, I was ready to tear my hair out in frustration. Even if I could correlate the information, I'd inevitably miss something. Even the most helpful site admitted that there was no way to be sure of the full extent of the faults. New fissures appeared all the time, many never even reaching the surface—until suddenly they did, swallowing someone's house, shearing off a section of cliff with an ocean view.

I pushed back from the computer, closed my eyes and tried *not* to think. My lightbulb moments usually came to me when I was in the middle of something else, a shower, a lonely stretch of road, allowing my mind to wander. Quiet moments hadn't exactly been plentiful recently.

Two things immediately pushed their way to the fore. One, the god-gossip website that mentioned the divinities making a comeback said something about old rivalries laid to rest for the sake of combining forces. In my limited experience, it took more than two to tango, conspiratorially speaking. Nothing in the Greco-Roman pantheon played quite as tight as sibling rivalry. If Poseidon Earthshaker had buried the hatchet with, say, Zeus Stormbringer or Hades...well, if he had a moniker, I'd never heard it...we were pretty much dead meat. Even two-thirds of the mighty triumvirate ought to be good for an apocalypse—or close enough for government work.

Second, my brain leapt to some new conclusions about Hermes's message. I'd been thinking about things all wrong. A cemetery plot didn't make any sense. Even a freshly dug hole wouldn't deliver explosives deeply enough into the earth to have a real impact. No, there was something else. I allowed my brain to wander over a mental map of L.A. until finally it clicked, panned right and zoomed in.

I was ready to burst when Armani knocked on the door seconds later. I flung it open and hugged him so hard I crushed the bag he carried.

"What's that for?"

I stepped back to look him in the eyes. "I *know*. I know where it's going to happen. Not when, but soon. Tomorrow, maybe. I think they're ready to make their big entrance."

His face was grim. "L.A.'s about to blow sky high and you're grinning like you've won the lottery."

That had better be some *good* chocolate he was carrying. "The point is, L.A.'s not going anywhere. We're going to stop it."

"How?"

My smile wobbled. "I haven't worked that part out yet. For that I need caloric fortification. What did you bring?"

"Eclairs, but they're probably flat now."

"They'll still taste the same. Come on in. What can I get you to drink with them? Coffee, milk?"

"Coffee, please."

I pulled him in, only then realizing we'd been talking about the end of L.A. right out in the hallway. My neighbors and I pretty much kept to ourselves, but I wondered if any had noticed the patrolman in the hall last night. If so, I hoped it hadn't made them particularly curious about the goings-on. Not that there was anything they or I could do about that.

I fiddled with the coffeepot, making enough to last a while. If we were going to come up with a plan, I needed all the artificial stimulation I could get.

"Okay, you've watched me sleep; you've seen me in a towel; you're no longer company. I'll pour, but you've got to do your own alchemy." I gave the sugar bowl a nudge along the counter.

Next thing I knew, Armani was right behind me, close enough that when he took a deep breath I felt his chest against my back. Then his hands were hot on my shoulders. My eyes closed and I leaned back into him, almost without thought. He slid one hand down my arm to my waist, then across my stomach to fan his hand there. My breath caught. He kissed the top of my head, which should have felt chaste but didn't, not with the warmth of his breath and his body pressed against mine. I wanted to turn toward him and try that kiss again, but I was afraid that if I moved it would break the spell and we'd find reason again to fight so that we could go back to our neutral corners. Which was just stupid. Were we so scared of losing a pointless flirtation that we'd sacrifice the chance for more? I couldn't speak for Armani, but for my part, hell—

I turned and his lips came down on mine. He must have started on his éclair; his lips were incredibly sweet. I wanted to lick them clean, but my lower lip was trapped between his teeth as he nibbled it until I moaned, then thrust his tongue into my mouth instead. For a moment we seemed to be fighting for dominance, his tongue parrying mine and falling back as I thrust into his mouth as well. Then he moved on to nip my earlobe as one hand traced my spine. I felt Armani growing against me and slid my hips back and forth against him. He groaned and started walking me back toward the bed.

I wanted him so badly that up against the kitchen counter would have been just fine with me, but at least this way I had the leisure to taste him, cup the butt I'd long admired, make him shake with need. I probably should have been thinking about ramifications, but if I was thinking at all, it was that I wanted to shake Armani's control, see him urgent with need. I wanted to feel those final hard thrusts before he spilled into me.

When he hit the bed, he pulled me down with him, then tried to roll me under. I stubbornly resisted, instead straddling him and riding his erection until he subsided with his hands on my hips, encouraging the motion. I was already wet and, if our clothes vanished in the next second, could easily take him, but that would be too quick. I pulled my camisole over my head and tossed it to the floor. Armani's eyes went straight to the black lace of my demi-cup bra.

"God, Tori." It sounded like it was forced out of him.

I leaned down, letting my breasts brush his chest, my nipples sensitive beneath the lace as I tasted his neck. In contrast to his lips, his neck was tangy, delicious. The taste made me shiver all the way down to where I rubbed against his erection.

With a hand to either side of my face, he raised my lips back to his, darting his tongue into my mouth, quick invasions that left me wanting more. No doubt that was the plan, as I let him roll me over a minute later so that he could devour my mouth while his hands alternately tweaked my nipples and caressed my flesh, above the bra, then down over it to my ribs and stomach on to the fastening of my slacks. He played with it for an exquisite second where I thought he would undo it and I'd finally get to feel him where I wanted him then settled for dipping his fingertips inside the waistband.

I freed my lips long enough to say, "Tease."

His gaze met mine. Inches away the blue was the color of midnight. "Not if I intend to follow through."

I slid a hand between us to cup his shaft, hot and rock hard, straining against the fabric barrier. "You're a little overdressed."

As he reached a hand down to remedy the situation, I felt a zing of another kind—danger. I gave an inarticulate cry as a thunderclap with the weight of a sonic boom startled the bejeebers out of me.

"What the hell!" Armani cursed.

"Get down!" I yelled.

Lightning lit the sky like a Roman candle. Armani and I dove for the floor, but the bolt was faster, shattering the window. Glass shards like missiles pierced my back as I fell. Wind whipped through the broken window, bringing with it a cold, driving rain. My back stung like a bundle of exposed nerves.

"You all right?" Armani called over the howling wind.

I didn't respond, teeth too tightly gritted against the pain as I reached for my shirt.

"Tori?" he prompted, an edge of concern creeping in.

"Hell no," I managed as the wave ebbed, "but there's—no time—for that. This has got to be the beginning... Too much power to waste all on us."

Another thunderclap sounded, rattling the remaining glass.

"Door. Now!" I yelled. To hell with my shirt.

Steeling myself, I gathered my strength and exploded up from the floor a millisecond before the second bolt destroyed my bed.

Armani beat me to the door and we thundered down the stairs, unwilling to trust the elevator's electrical system. I was more gasping than breathing, praying under my breath that the glass shards in my back wouldn't sever anything vital. Already the pain signals were so scrambled my whole body felt aflame. Armani burst out onto the street first and hit the auto-unlock on his car. I threw myself into the back as he slammed into the driver's seat.

"What—" he swiveled to look at me, eyes going wide at my prone position—or maybe it was all the blood.

"Just drive!" I ordered.

The agony of twisting to close the door nearly blacked me out. I steadied myself with my hands as best I could, trying to anticipate the jolts while spots danced before my eyes. At least I was too distracted to worry about the fact that I was naked from the waist up.

"Where?" he asked.

"Tar pits. Call Lau, call anyone you think will listen. We're going to need reinforcements."

The wind shrieked around the car. Rain hit with such force it sounded like hail. I could practically feel Armani fighting for control of the car. Maybe dividing his attention with the phone wasn't such a hot idea.

"Never mind." A sudden bump in the road made me wince. "Pass the phone to me."

"You can barely talk."

"Screw that. You need to focus."

Armani grabbed the phone from its belt holster; I was amazed I hadn't dislodged it back at my place. He handed it back to me without turning around.

My back twinged as I took it, but the pain, weirdly, seemed very far away, which was either a miracle or a really, really bad sign. I flexed my feet—thank gods, still working.

I called Lau, told her about the tar pits, everything. Let her call the cavalry. If anyone was likely to mobilize troops, I was betting on her.

Another thunderclap rumbled and lightning turned night into day. A huge CR-RACK! sounded and Armani cursed as a giant palm tree began to topple. He slammed on the brakes, but not soon enough. Impact took the front bumper and smashed the lights, but at least we were still alive.

"You've got sucky aim, buddy!" Armani yelled at the sky. He hit reverse. The car protested, leaving some of itself behind, but finally let go with a giant groan of metal. "Hang on!"

Armani did a crazy U-turn that almost spun us three-hundred-and-sixty degrees before he got control and headed for a detour. The move would nearly have killed me moments ago. Now—

I tentatively sat up. The tinkling of falling glass joined the howling chorus of the elements. I brushed it away, onto the floor and felt my back. Raised welts. That was all. My body had rejected the glass, knit itself together. About as natural as the storm raging outside.

Armani flicked a glance at me in the rearview mirror.

"What the hell?"

"Don't ask." *'Cause I don't know*, I thought. I was guessing Apollo had a lot to answer for, though in this case I couldn't get all worked up over it.

"Okay, how about this one: why the tar pits? How do you know?"

"Hermes." Had I told him about Hermes? In all the insanity, I couldn't remember. "I tracked him down. All he gave me was, 'I hope you don't unearth the plot too late.'"

"Based on that—"

"Hey, give me some credit, okay? I grew up with the tales. I know how these things work. It took me a while to figure it out. At first I thought he was talking about a cemetery plot, but that didn't make sense with the whole earthquake/explosives plan we'd figured on. Graves just don't go deep enough. But the tar pits make all kinds of sense—deep, open fissures the tar still bubbles up through to the surface, excavations all over the place and, if you think of it the right way, a graveyard. Animals, even a woman, went in but they never came out, except as fossils."

"I hope you're right."

"So do I."

"Are you going to call Apollo?" he asked.

I crawled through the space between seats so that I could sit up front. He looked over quickly, but I noticed his eyes made a quick stop at my chest before moving up to my face.

"Do you want me to?" I asked.

"It wouldn't hurt to have a—uh—god on our side."

The car hydroplaned and Armani fought for control. I grabbed the handrest, as if that would save me. Armani cursed fluently as the car spun a one-eighty, making geysers of the water on either side of us. He steered into the turn until we were facing the way we'd come.

While he righted us, I pried my fingers off the handrest to reach for my seat belt.

"I don't think his powers are really, um, warlike," I said feebly.

Armani risked another glance away from the road. "Oh, really? Never mind. I don't want to know. Maybe he's got friends."

Yeah, but which side would they be on? If it came down to gods bent on recovering their power against humans who'd really rather they didn't, which side would Apollo choose? What in the world did we have to offer?

On the flip side, *not* calling Apollo had never kept him out of the loop before.

"The storm seems to be moving off in the direction we're headed, like it's got something else on the agenda."

"Good. If it has to give up battering us to focus elsewhere, maybe the gods only have enough power for one small concentrated storm. Maybe we can wear them out." I wondered how long they could keep it going fueled only by the belief of Yiayia and a few other eccentrics. "The bad news is that with lightning et. al., we may be facing Zeus as well as Poseidon and Hephaestus."

"Fantastic. Can't wait. Call Apollo."

Right...but with Apollo's ability to scry me and all—"Um, Armani, you got something I can wear?"

His lips tugged upward in a lascivious grin. "You're a better distraction as you are now."

"*Please.*"

"In the back, I think maybe there's a jacket."

I reached behind the seats and found the jacket on the floor behind Armani, where I'd probably pushed it in my graceful belly slide into the backseat. Or, I thought when I held it closer and caught a whiff, it had been there for a really, really long time. Still, it probably wouldn't bite and I was in no position to be choosy. I put it on, zipped it up and rolled the sleeves thrice.

Then I dialed Apollo, but with no idea what to say that wouldn't make me sound like a whack job if anyone else checked his messages—like the police in the event he'd already become a casualty. My heart clenched. I hung up when his voice mail kicked in. If he was interested, my number would come up as a missed call.

"No luck," I reported.

"Plan?" he asked.

"I'm open to suggestions."

"Great."

I couldn't say for sure, with the raindrops still committing hari-kari on our windshield, but I thought I spotted the entrance to Hancock Park, the tar pit complex, just ahead. Yup, no mistaking the stylized saber-tooth tiger guarding the gate, even with our headlights the park's only illumination. It was eerily dark. No security lights. No street lamps lit in the vicinity. Nada. Armani pulled into one of the empty spaces all around the business district this time of night.

"What do you want to bet this freak storm has cut power to annoying little things like alarm systems?" Armani asked.

"And backup generators. Don't suppose you have any night-vision goggles."

Armani snorted. "Flashlight in the glove compartment and some flares in the trunk, that's about it."

"Gun?" I asked, reaching into the glove box to grab said light and trying to ignore Armani's stare.

"Where's yours?"

"Lockbox at home," I answered defensively. "I didn't exactly have time to grab it."

No need for him to know I hadn't used it since—

An immense gust actually lifted the car up on two wheels and dropped us down again. *Damn*, we had regained the storm's attention.

"No safer in than out," I said, mostly to psych myself up. "Let's do it."

Armani nodded and we threw open the doors—or tried to. The wind hurled the door back in my face, but my shoulder took the brunt of the impact. Hard rain picked up the slack, stinging like ice—or acid. I could see only the narrowest sliver of world through my eyes, squinting to near blindness in defense against the burn. A thunderclap clashed with enough force to crack my chattering teeth together. "Get away from the car," Armani yelled.

"Trying!"

I took a deep breath and channeled my inner strongman, er, woman. "Eee-yah!" With a sudden burst of power, I flung the door back at the wind and pounded pavement. My feet nearly went out from under me on the slick street, but I managed to right myself and make it to Armani's side. I held the flashlight and he the gun as we advanced on the gate, blinking against the rain that threatened to eat us alive.

A bolt had melted the gate to slag. The flashlight beam didn't extend beyond, so it was impossible to see what lay in wait. We'd ditched the car so quickly that the flares still sat uselessly in the trunk. We'd be blind to anything more than a few steps away. We took those steps, over the twisted lump that had once guarded the complex from trespassers like us. Then we crept a few more paces across the grass, toward the slowly bubbling morass of tar and groundwater that I knew from past visits held plaster representations of mammoths soon to become one with the earth.

Those few steps had brought us to the eye of the storm, the eerie oasis of calm around which everything swirled. As I panned the flashlight beam before us, I knew why. A chill skittered up my spine as the beam hit upon the figure in profile to us a quarter of the way around the lake—powerful build, high-tech goggles and a faintly glowing remote. Hiero—no, call him what he was at that moment—Hephaestus, deranged god of the forge. The beam of my light tore his focus away from the black water. He thrust one arm out at me and the bulb in the flashlight blew. Darkness swallowed us.

Chapter Sixteen

"Nightmares are what happen when the gods open up your skull, scramble your deepest darkest fears and play them back to you in a Quentin Tarantino-inspired montage."

—*Tori Karacis*

"Now would be a good time for those flares," I said, reaching out for Armani's hand, not because I was suddenly scared that all my worst fears were about to come true, but to assure that we wouldn't get separated.

"You want to go back for them, be my guest."

Even amidst the chaos I spared a millisecond to appreciate that he didn't coddle me, even as on some level it pissed me off.

"Well then?" I asked.

"Hey, this is your show."

I thought quickly. Thick dark clouds still blocked light from the stars, moon, and distant glow of the unaffected part of the city. I wondered if there'd be enough light from the readout on Hephaestus's remote for me to give him the gorgon glare and put him out of commission. First, though, I'd have to get close.

"Nick, count to ten, then start a distraction. Fire at Hephaestus, whatever you have to do, but keep his attention on you. I'm going to try to get close."

He grabbed my hand as I tried to lift it away.

"What?" I asked in irritation, wondering if he was belatedly about to go all he-man chivalrous on me.

"You called me Nick."

"So?" The name had slipped out like some deathbed confession. I didn't want to analyze it or the analogy I'd just made.

"Nothing," he said, voice hard. "Go."

I did, hoping there'd be time to make it up to Nick—*Armani*—later.

Running as fast as I could on the wet ground, I had to trust my memory of the layout. I circled well away from the tar pit to sneak up behind Hephaestus. The only point of reference I had was the faint glow of the remote. Once he eclipsed it, I was set.

Armani started his hue and cry, but in the midst of the whipping wind, it was a pretty pitiful display. Hephaestus didn't even twitch as he micro-focused on the remote—a guidance system for sending the explosives down into the faults? I hadn't considered the environmental handicap of my slap-dash plan.

A siren wailed across the night and blue fought red for the spotlight. Over the downed gate I could see a patrol car fishtail down the road and felt the wind shift, as if the storm had just turned its attention that way. The sky split open above me and another flashbulb fried the air, ripping toward the car. Two things happened instantaneously—the car spun out and the bolt hit home, shattered the headlights, which cracked, popped and died, and lifted the car off the ground. Figures hurled themselves out of either side of the vehicle, one Lau's compressed aggression and the other a blur of uniform. My first

198

thought was to run to them, but my second was that the Fates had finally leered in my direction.

In Hephaestus's appreciation of the moment, he wasn't paying attention to much else. I closed the distance in ground-eating strides and launched myself at him in a flying tackle. My arms latched onto his neck and shoulders. He gave a roar that could shake mountains and a great heave, as though he could just shrug me off. Surprised at my own strength, I held on even when he shook like a mastiff fending off a beagle pup too big for its britches. I was squeezing so hard my chest ached at the effort of expanding while squashed flat against his back.

Finally, *finally*, he did as I'd hoped, dropped the remote to deal with me. He reached huge hands to pry me off, but I folded like a cheap suit, all the way to the ground, and landed in a crouch. With my outstretched leg, I swept the remote into the pit in a move resembling the coffee grinder it was named for, glad my circus training hadn't been completely for naught. The remote's glow cut off abruptly and the world went black.

Hephaestus growled. I tried to steel myself for the blow that was sure to come. Those glasses, I suspected, were for night vision, and Hephaestus was the one goggled man in the country of the blind. The blow didn't fall, and that worried me more. Was it possible the remote was not the only way to control the charges? I nearly smacked my head against the ground in frustration. Of course there'd be redundancies. They'd had ages to plan. I just had to hope that Hephaestus and the others wouldn't set the charges off while the god was still in range. We'd been running on a wing and a prayer the gods were disinclined to answer.

Well, bumbling around in the dark had gotten me this far; I couldn't stop now for fear of a little thing like becoming part of the fossil record.

I rose like a whirling dervish, just in case Hephaestus was in range. The odd calm of the storm suddenly broke again, and I screamed as it lashed me across the face with a stinging backhanded blow. My eyes burned, tears poured ineffectually down my face, and my throat closed off.

I flung my arms up to protect against a second onslaught, but that was the end. Hope bloomed that it had just been the recoil of the gods letting go of the storm, but the hope was short-lived.

Flares fired up, casting a red glow over the field of battle.

"Hands up!" Lau yelled, as soon as she could see well enough to get a bead on Hephaestus.

He ripped the goggles off his face before complying with a smile worthy of Charles or maybe Marilyn Manson.

I waited for him to fire off some pithy catchphrase of villainy, but his statement was a little more physical.

A sharp-edged crash split the night, coming from the Page Museum. I turned instinctively toward the sound and was grabbed roughly from behind in a full nelson. It almost didn't matter. Standing amidst the razor shards of shattered museum glass were two beasts of another age: a saber-toothed cat and a giant ground sloth. My brain stuttered over the vision, unable to process until my eyes fixed on those places where the glass had shorn away fake fur to expose the animatronic innards. The display models that battled it out day after day in the tar pit museum had come to life.

"The girl and I will be leaving," Hephaestus yelled. "My toys will make sure the rest of you don't get any ideas."

Girl? Girl!

I stomped down on his insole, popped my elbow into his solar plexus and bent, ready to throw him over my shoulder, only he never buckled. That was *it*. I went all alley cat, scratching, shrieking, clawing, kicking, anything to gain enough slack to stone the bastard. He was ready for me this time, lifting me off my feet and shaking me until my brain rattled around in my skull.

"Stop," he commanded.

"We're dead anyway!" I yelled to the others.

"As you wish," he snarled.

In a blur of speed, the prehistoric beasts were upon Armani and the others. Gunshots cracked. Still I saw the smilodon's huge jaws unhinge and snap down around the defensive arm Armani had lifted. He screamed, and I yelled with him. The sloth battled Lau and the patrolman as easily as a bear swatting flies, batting them to the ground. I didn't see the officer rise again. Lau laid where she'd fallen, still firing off shots.

"No!" I shouted, but Hephaestus just laughed and moved us past the slaughter, out toward the street and escape.

Apollo! I shouted mentally, knowing it wouldn't work, that even if in the crazy new world order he heard me, he'd never reach us in time.

But I was wrong. He was already there. Right in front of us, menacing and deadly serious with an arrow aimed at Hephaestus's head, which I was too short to shield. Oddly, Apollo didn't look at all out of place with the archaic weapon. He looked more—just *more*—than he'd ever been before. Larger. More present. I'd forgotten that the hunter was one of his aspects.

"Call them off," he said.

Hephaestus didn't jump to. "Do you really want to set yourself against us?" he asked.

"I said *call them off.*" I bit off each word.

I felt Hephaestus's shrug and the sudden susurrus of sound behind us.

"You've signed your own death warrant," Hephaestus snarled.

Ah, finally, the villainous one-liner. Sadly not witty enough to appreciate, especially without knowing the fate of those on the ground.

"This is not the way," Apollo answered, arrow unwavering. "There are far more of them than there are of us. Make them fear you and they will hunt you down."

"Hah! Teach them to fear and the smart ones will ally themselves with us. Our worship will be restored. We will have the power to crush the others."

"We'll just have to agree to disagree. Let her go."

"You always did have the low-brow taste for human flesh."

Apollo refused to be baited. "Let her go. This is the last time I will repeat myself for you."

"Yes," Hephaestus answered, "it is."

I couldn't tell what happened next. Apollo released a shaft. A jagged bolt of lightning streaked from the sky. No forks, no dramatically beautiful strike, just a single focused pulse headed right for Apollo. Hephaestus jerked me skyward as a shield against the hunter's arrow, but too slowly. The indescribable sound of the shaft imbedding in flesh, Hephaestus's roar of pain, the awful spurting of blood, my bone-jarring impact with the ground as Hephaestus's grip went slack all seemed to happen at once. Skewers of pain shot through my legs.

From the heap I'd fallen into I looked up to meet two sets of inhuman eyes nearly glowing with life. Hephaestus fell behind me, but I could hear him flailing around, grunting and panting with pain. Not dead yet. I only hoped the same could be said for my friends.

Apollo lay still as death a few yards away. The smell of charred flesh met the coppery smell of blood and the asphalt/sour-pickle scent of the bubbling tar from the pits. A cry caught in my throat and my knees shrieked as I tried to get them to bear my weight, carry me toward him.

At the motion, the animatronic monsters sprang. The smilodon hit first. Pain ripped through my knees as I dodged, not entirely successful. Steel claws tore through muscles and tendons, shredding my shoulder, exposing nerves left raw and screaming. I managed to keep my feet, but just barely. The beasts circled, squeezing me between them and the tar pits. An idea formed through the haze of pain, to use my body as the red flag in a game of matador. If I could stay alive long enough, maybe the tar pit would finish them off just as it had their extinct forbearers.

The sloth nearly blindsided me. Only that precognitive tingle of danger let me pivot in time to avoid the crushing blow. It brought me dangerously close to the pit; not so the sloth that veered at the last moment, faster than it looked. I was going to have to time everything just right or one flying tackle would put me over the edge. The smilodon didn't wait for his partner to get into position before launching his attack, but the sloth was only microseconds behind, closing from a converging angle. My head swiveled from the smilodon's blade-like teeth gleaming wet and red to the sloth's massive claws.

I waited until every instinct I had screamed at me to run, then ducked and rolled beneath their lunging claws, but I'd overestimated the aerodynamics of robotic ground sloths. The beast's hind feet came down on my back. Something snapped. Pain bloomed like a mushroom cloud. The world went supernova.

Then the earth itself exploded. Hot tar shot into the sky, the turf bucked like a goosed bull. I curled into a fetal ball to present the least surface area to the heated debris. Through the haze of pain and misery, I registered distantly that the quake hadn't been as bad as it could have been, that maybe we'd stopped Hephaestus from setting the charges deeply enough. Then I felt something grab hold of all that force and *heave.*

Suddenly my teeth cracked together with enough force to splinter, and I felt like I was being shaken apart. The whole earth was coming apart at the seams.

A crack started off to my side. Whatever damage the sloth had done to my back, I couldn't wait for it to heal, even assuming that earlier incident with the glass hadn't been a freak thing. My breath stalled as I bit back the pain, but I got to one knee before I had to stop and steady myself. The world doubled, tripled, divided into a myriad blurring images. Beneath me the earth continued to heave, and I tacked like a ship at sea trying to get to my feet.

Two other forms rose—Hephaestus and Apollo. The sight kicked me in the chest. Apollo *alive.*

"Run!" I yelled, as if they couldn't figure that out, but they were too focused on each other.

And also the least of my worries. They could survive electrocution and arrows through the neck—for all I knew everything short of having their hearts ripped out like Circe. I left them to it. Jagged blades of pain ripped through me at every step, but I rode the tremors, letting them propel me toward Armani and Lau.

In the distance, a second quake seemed to overlay the first, and an animal cry of anguish cut across the night, even over the rumble of the quake, striking dread into my heart. Some primal part of me recognized it, though I'd never heard its like before. The dragon. He was awake and he was *Pissed*.

Lau's head snapped up, and she wavered to hands and knees. Armani and the young patrolman still hadn't moved, and now I knew why. The patrolman didn't have a throat left. His head and shoulders were only connected by the thinnest bloody filaments of flesh. Bile rose up in my throat and threatened to spill over.

I turned fearfully toward Armani, who looked little better. There was so much blood coating his chest, I was afraid he was dead. I couldn't see where the wounds were; there was just too much gore. But Atropos hadn't yet cut the cord of his life. His chest still rose and fell.

"All right, you bastards," I yelled at the sky. "Show your cowardly asses so I can kick them back to Olympus."

"What are you doing?" Lau hissed.

I was too angry to consider the wisdom of taunting gods with firebolts.

"Come on, you *malakas*, come out from behind your damned storm—or don't you think you can take me? Look," I took off the jacket I'd borrowed from Armani and hurled it at the sky, "I'm unarmed. You want me, you'd better damn well get down here and finish the job. If I live the world will know you weren't man enough to take me."

"Tori!" Apollo's voice was muffled by Hephaestus's hand on his face as they grappled like boys on the ground, more schoolyard brawl now that they'd both lost their weapons than Hollywood god on god action.

A cloud burst above and hard rain fell impressively, building figures from the ground up.

"Now what?" Lau asked, disgusted.

"Take Armani and go. Get him to the hospital. I'll keep them focused on me."

"Throw yourself to the wolves—good plan. You are crazy."

"It helps. Now *go!*"

I stood fast, watching Lau strain to lift Armani's greater weight and flexing my back to be sure it wouldn't give me any nasty surprises when the time came to move. Whatever super-healing thing Apollo had done was kick-ass. I wasn't one hundred percent, but I could breathe through the pain.

Both of the gelling gods snarled at me as their forms solidified. It was the first time I'd seen either in the flesh, as it were. Zeus was Wolverine on a really bad hair day. Poseidon looked, well, like something out of *Clash of the Titans* or a really brawny midshipman who'd climbed the rigging to yell defiance at the storm. Once I pushed my overactive imagination down deep and forced myself to focus, I could tell they were tired. Bags under their eyes, a certain slump to their stance—as if that would give me a chance.

Freeze! I shouted mentally, putting everything I had behind it—pain, rage, fear. It wasn't enough. Neither would meet my eyes. I muttered about damned useless talents and flew into action, squatting to pick up a clod of wet dirt to toss in their faces, then dropping again to avoid retaliation and sweep a leg outward to take them off their feet. The clod hit Zeus, who wheeled away, outside the range of my swipe, which did catch the mighty Poseidon. The earth shuddered again at his fall, and he gave a great woof of pain, but my eyes were on the god still standing.

Zeus recovered, turned on me with eyes blazing and hands flexing.

"You *dare?*"

"I didn't know truth was an option," I retorted, just in case the question hadn't been rhetorical.

He growled and flew at me like a linebacker going for a flying tackle. I dodged and he landed hard on one shoulder, rolling awkwardly to one side.

"Russian judge gives that one a 2.0," I said.

Zeus forgot himself long enough to glare right at me, and I hit him again with my whammy. *Freeze!* This time he did.

Then I was airborne, all the air knocked out of me by the force of a body hitting mine at mach eight. The impact with the ground had barely registered on my pain-meter before Poseidon's weight added to the splintering pain in my back and arms, which had done most of the catching. I wanted to elbow him in the face, throw him off, but I didn't think I could move. Something had snapped, crackled and popped. My ears roared and my vision went hazy with whatever natural drug my body was pumping to combat the pain.

"Got you," he breathed into my ear, the smell of brine and decomping fish wafting with it.

I went limp, playing possum and praying he wouldn't make me roadkill. He bought it, allowed himself to shift enough to wrap his arms around my head, the better to snap my neck. The movement had freed one of my legs. Just the opening I needed. Anchoring my hips into the ground, I flung the freed leg up toward my back—or rather, the one in the way of mine—with my hard heel aimed to maim. The heel landed a sharp blow to Poseidon's coccyx just as his arms began to tighten. His body spasmed in reaction to the pain, knocking him off me, and bringing us nearly face-to-face.

"Poseidon!" I snapped. Pain-filled eyes instinctively met mine. "Freeze!"

He did.

I looked toward Apollo, who seemed to be locked in a permanent clinch with Hephaestus. They'd wrestled to a stalemate. Whoever passed out first lost.

I rose, spikes of pain shooting up my arms. Something was broken; fractured at the very least, but slowly and painfully my limbs obeyed my commands. I searched the patrolman for his zip-tie cuffs and tucked them and his weapon into my jeans. The ties were for the downed gods. The gun for Hephaestus.

I walked over to the struggling gods and pointed the gun toward Hephaestus's head at point-blank range. That froze him even without my mojo.

"You twitch that finger, girlie, and all I have to do is roll your boyfriend into position."

I shrugged, "Through him or around him, you'll still be dead. Long as I miss his heart, I'm figuring he'll recover. But you I won't be aiming to miss. On target or not, you'll pass out sooner or later and then I'll have you."

"Bitch."

"Ooh, good comeback, but nobody said you could call me by my first name. Now, release Apollo."

Apollo eyed me like he was ready to fight me next. He caught the zip-tie I tossed at him with a glare that let me know where he'd plant an arrow if only he hadn't lost them all in the quake.

"Relax," I said, as soon as Hephaestus was secured, "it was a bluff."

"I'll laugh later," he answered stiffly.

"That's all I ask."

I felt my shoulders sag in relief. It was *over*. Really over. We'd defeated three of the most powerful gods of old. I'd pirouette if only I had the energy left. Okay, maybe not. A long soak and a good sleep seemed more the thing. But first there was the little problem of what to do with our captives.

"What the hell do we do with these three?" I asked Apollo. "Free they'll be gunning for me, but I don't think the police can hold them once their powers have recharged. I don't want anyone to get hurt."

He looked at me, still pissed, but one side of his mouth started to twitch with some secret amusement.

"Come on, share," I said.

"You think Homeland Security has a contingency plan for *this*?"

Hephaestus spat at that thought, but we both ignored him.

"Why don't we find out? If you'll do guard duty, I'll find a nice anonymous pay phone and call it in. I don't want HS to trace anything back to me and get all forgetful about my personal freedoms because they don't like my answers to their questions."

"Fair enough."

I put a hand to his cheek, silently thanking him for his timely arrival, and realized that my back didn't so much as twinge. Grateful as I was, it reminded me that I still had questions of my own.

"What did you do to me anyway? What's with this superhero healing thing I've got going on?"

Apollo grimaced, and his eyes skidded off to the side.

I tapped his cheek to bring his focus back to me. "*Apollo.*"

He met my gaze only reluctantly. "Ambrosia, food of the gods. The other day when you were kidnapped, you were in really bad shape. I wasn't sure you were going to make it; it was the only way I knew to help."

"*And—*"

"And what?"

"And you didn't tell me because... Wait, ambrosia...tell me we're not talking immortality here."

Again his eyes slid away from mine. Oh, this was bad. "Not yet; not from one dose."

"Then what's the downside?"

"You're going to want more."

"Hell yes, you ought to bottle the stuff."

He didn't even crack a smile. The hand I'd stopped him with formed a claw. "Wait, by 'want', you mean 'need', don't you? Like an addict."

He finally looked me in the eye. "Yes."

I saw red, great glaring blood-washed crimson.

"I'm going to go now. I need to hit something and right now it's you."

"Tori—" He reached out to me.

"No!" I roared. My body shook with the effort to hold myself back.

Fists clenched at my side, I pivoted toward the gate and stalked off. He'd saved my life, a small part of me insisted. More than once, it said. But it wasn't the part that was winning. Rationally, unemotionally, that was probably true, but I'd watched Pappous struggle with alcohol his whole life, falling off the wagon, clawing his way out, falling again. I'd vowed addiction would *never* rule my life. Nothing was ever going to control me. I felt like my freedom, my independence, had been stripped away, and I was now slave to a *substance*. For all I knew, to Apollo too, as my pusher. It wasn't as if it was something I could obtain at any corner store. I had no idea if ambrosia withdrawal was survivable, but I intended to find out.

What really made me mad was that I'd known, *known* I couldn't trust him and done it anyway. I'd thought I was still resisting, but I was wrong. That made me culpable as well.

Still seeing red, I barely registered picking my way over cracks and debris and using directory assistance to place the call to Homeland Security. I did retain enough presence of mind to use the jacket sleeves to hold the receiver and to dial. I knew they'd trace the phone and didn't want my prints anywhere in evidence. The man I spoke with wasn't nearly finished with me when I hung up. I felt a certain satisfaction that I was leaving Apollo to deal with them. Poetic justice, in a sense.

Drained now, it was all I could do to walk back to the cars so that I could vacate the area. It suddenly dawned on me that the one vehicle I had was Armani's and I was keyless. Uncle Christos had taught me how to hot-wire a car. I could only hope I remembered.

I had to fight to stay awake on the drive back to my apartment. Going on autopilot was not going to get me around the downed trees and power lines that littered the roadway in the wake of the quake. I wanted to go right to the hospital to check on Armani, but in my state, covered in mud and blood, they'd likely mistake me for a patient. I'd had enough well-intentioned biological tinkering to last me a lifetime.

I saw the flashing red lights from two streets away and knew with a sick certainty exactly what I'd find when I turned my corner. A fireman with a light stick diverted traffic a few blocks from my building. Smoke rose thick into the air. Unable to process any more blows, I parked on a side street and walked zombie-like as far as the barricades would let me go. My building was up in flames, fully involved or however they put it. That second bolt of lightning we'd ducked out on must have started a fire. And with no one around to put it out...

My knees buckled and I fell to the sidewalk. Everything I had, gone. I'd lived too seat-of-my-pants for renter's insurance. No, I'd trusted the Fates. I was about ready to pound my forehead on the concrete when I realized I wasn't alone. One of the onlookers, radiating concern, asked if she could help.

I summoned a weak smile for her. "No, thanks."

Once again I mustered the strength to move when I was well past the point of collapse and shuffled dejectedly toward Armani's car, where silent tears streaked down my face until I fell asleep.

Chapter Seventeen

"It's all over but the end."
—*one of Pappous's favorite sayings*

I woke up, feeling like a rag someone had wrung out and left to stiffen in the overnight chill. For a moment I was so focused on my aches and pains that nothing else registered. Then the morning light shining in my face, my bursting bowels and the fact that I was IN A CAR made an impression. I was homeless.

I checked my pockets for essentials, hoping I'd at least retained an ATM card. My cell phone was AWOL, but other than that I seemed to be equipped to at least prove my identity, shop and get into my office. A tear leaked out when I touched my house keys, and I brushed it away. I tried to tell myself it was just stuff, but among that stuff had been the charm bracelet my parents had given me for high school graduation, which I hardly ever wore because it got in my way, but which meant a lot to me all the same. It had a charm for every part I'd ever played—a hand for palmistry, a tumbler for acrobatics... There was more too, posters from various venues, photographs, letters. It felt like even the remnants of my former life had been burned away.

Bad enough I could never return; now I couldn't so much as look back.

I shook it off. There were things to do. Yiayia was going to go frantic when she heard the news through whatever local feed had ratted me out so far. I needed to find a phone, wash up, change, eat and get some blessed caffeine—not necessarily in that order.

My car was parked in front of my building. After a quick drive by to see that it, at least, had been spared, I headed for the office. A tiny paranoid part of me that hadn't existed just a week ago whispered that my car might not be safe, and pre-coffee I didn't trust myself to make sure, so I just continued on to my office without swapping vehicles. I hoped to find a change of clothes tucked away in my gym bag, since I'd already used my spare suit, and a shallow sink where I could do a cursory wash-up.

For the first time I was thankful our poor old office building didn't have a doorman. *I* wouldn't have let me up, covered in dirt and blood. Jesus crossed himself as I entered, but said nothing beyond, "*Madre de Dio.*"

"Do we have anything in petty cash?" I asked.

"I think so."

"Great, would you order us in some breakfast? Make it continental. I feel the need for carbs. And espresso."

"Sure, boss."

I dragged myself to my office and locked the door behind me. Fifteen minutes later my hair still smelled like smoke and my clothes like clean, honest sweat, but I looked marginally presentable.

"Sit," Jesus ordered as I emerged.

He must have moved heaven and earth to get a delivery so quickly, but already he had a plate stacked for me with a pastry and an espresso lightened to latte.

"You're a lifesaver," I said in a hush, falling into the client chair and taking a huge sip of espresso before anything else.

He eyed me over his own cardboard cup. "Your aunt has called three times."

"I'll call her."

He nodded. "A check and letter came for you this morning by courier. I take it you solved Circe's murder. Was it the strange man they fished out of the ocean in Santa Monica?"

I'd gulped the rest of my latte already and made it through a pastry and a half, but stopped, queasy and still hungry all at the same time.

"Letter?"

"From the studpuppy."

My bruised brain took a moment to process that he was talking about Apollo. My words for him were not nearly so complimentary.

"Oh, sure," I answered, keeping my face blank. "Go ahead and deposit the check. I think I promised you dinner and an explanation. But I'm, ah, going to have to do a little shopping first. Tonight? Anywhere you want to go—within reason," I added, as his eyes lit up. "There are probably a few things you should know." Especially if anyone in an official capacity came calling about what happened at the pits.

"I'll clear my schedule."

"Any chance I can borrow your cell phone for the day?"

He eyed me suspiciously. "What happened to *your* phone?"

"Up in smoke. You didn't see my building fire on the news this morning?"

"My god, *chica*, the way you came in—yesterday's clothes, all war-torn, I was thinking rave."

I cracked a smile, felt like the first in days. "Thank you for your estimation of my social life. Phone?"

He handed it over reluctantly. "No roaming."

Illegal as it was without a headset, I called Yiayia on the way to the hospital. I didn't want to spare the time to stop off just to get chewed out. I stayed on only long enough to assure her I was fine and would call later. She was going to make me pay for signing off while she was just winding up.

I had to go through the whole rigmarole of showing ID and getting checked off an approved list just to get in to see Armani. Apparently, one way or another he'd been connected with last night's devastation at the tar pits and environs and everyone was being careful until they knew exactly what was what. I wished them luck sorting it out.

I stood in the doorway of his hospital room for a minute just watching him watch the wall-mounted television. He looked good. Tired, ashen, but alive. I wanted to—the wave of emotion that swept over me was nearly ludicrous—I wanted to climb in next to him and do things worthy of a true-confessions cover story.

"You're alive," he said, turning carefully to look at me. "Thank God."

"Which one?" I asked, embarrassed he'd caught me starring. "You're looking good."

He snorted. "Liar."

"Okay, you look like you'll recover, which is a helluva lot better than you looked last time I saw you."

"Stop, you'll make me blush."

"That's the plan. You're not getting rid of me until you have to toddle down the hall to the facilities and I sneak a peek at you in your backless gown."

"Not gonna happen."

"We'll see."

We soaked up the silence for a moment, studying each other. It was more comfortable than I'd thought it would be.

"I heard about your apartment building," he said finally. "I'm sorry."

I looked away from his brilliant blue eyes then to pull the visitor's chair toward his bed. "Yeah, well, just don't tell anyone from zoning I'm sleeping at the office for the foreseeable future."

"You can probably take Lau's place. She's gone. Gonna need a caretaker."

His gaze had shifted toward the window, as if he looked to find her there.

"Gone where?"

"After the dragon. Just after she dropped me at the ER. Said something about a sacred trust."

"Great. Now all we need is a Knight Templar and a secret code and our picture is complete."

"I hope you're planning to knock on wood, because the way things have been going—"

My incipient grin widened into a huge yawn.

"You got room in that bed for me?" I asked. "I sort of passed out in your car last night. Not really conducive to sleep. I'm stiff as a board."

"I think that's supposed to be my line."

"Well, if you'd shove over, I could climb in and see for myself."

My eyes widened as his went all come-hither.

"You can't possibly be in any position to—"

"Well, we'll have to be careful and you'll have to do something about that privacy curtain."

I must have stared.

"You're doing that speechless thing again. I'm going to have to keep this up."

I ripped the pastel plaid curtain shut. "I'm calling your bluff."

"Go for it."

Which was how I found out exactly how much could and couldn't be done in a hospital bed with an injured cop who gave new meaning to the word "patient".

Sometime later, after falling sleep in a very unusual position, I beat a hasty retreat when an embarrassed-sounding nurse called from the other side of the curtain, "Um, Mr. Armani, time for your pain meds."

I inadvertently prodded Armani in a very bad place in my hurry to get out, replace and right clothing. I apologized softly and escaped, avoiding the nurse's stare on my way out. I ducked into the guest bathroom down the hallway and caught my reflection in the mirror. Oh, that nurse knew exactly what had gone on. If the rumpled clothing hadn't given it away, my tangled hair and rueful but satisfied smile would have done the trick.

I tried to tamp down on that smile, but it was no use. It was irrepressible. And dammit, I deserved irrepressible after the week I'd had. I ducked into one of the stalls and heard something crinkle as I prepared to sit.

Apollo's letter. Funny that I hadn't been reminded earlier.

A sudden prickle of unease went through me, and I wanted to toss it, forget everything I knew of gods and other insanity, but there was a curious bit of longing beneath that. I tried to tell myself it was just the extra kick of power and excitement that comes of being "in" on something most people don't even know exists and not for the man himself. Not after what he'd done. Besides, there was Armani now, and I was not cut out for intrigue or love triangles. I still needed some answers Apollo could provide. In the end, though, none of the justifications mattered. I was curious. Satisfaction was a flap-flip away.

The stationary was textured and pale, what Jesus would probably call "eggshell". Lifting the flap revealed scarlet foil and a single sheet of notepaper.

For some reason, I hesitated before sliding the card out of the pocket. It held only two words.

I KNOW.

I had a feeling that while the battle was over, the war had just begun.

About the Author

Lucienne Diver does not actually come from circus folk, though you'd never know it to meet her family. She is, however, in no particular order, a wife, mother, book addict, sun-worshipper, mythology enthusiast, beader, travel-junkie, clothes horse and crazy person. She writes the *Vamped* series of young adult novels for Flux Books (www.fluxnow.com), which School Library Journal calls, "a lighthearted, action-packed, vampire romance story following in the vein of Julie Kenner's 'Good Ghouls' (Berkley), Marlene Perez's 'Dead' (Harcourt), and Rachel Caine's 'The Morganville Vampires' (Signet) series." Her short stories have been included in the *Strip-Mauled* and *Fangs for the Mammaries* anthologies edited by Esther Friesner, and her essay "Abuse" is included in the 2011 anthology *Dear Bully*. Further information is available on her website, www.luciennediver.com, and on her blog, www.luciennediver.wordpress.com. You can also follow her on Twitter, @LucienneDiver.

The first bullet is always free. After that, you gotta pay.

The Zero Dog War
© 2011 Keith Melton

After accidentally blowing up both a client facility and a cushy city contract in the same day, pyromancer and mercenary captain Andrea Walker is scrambling to save her Zero Dogs. A team including (but not limited to) a sexually repressed succubus, a werewolf with a thing for health food, a sarcastic tank driver/aspiring romance novelist, a three-hundred-pound calico cat, and a massive demon who really loves to blow stuff up.

With the bankruptcy vultures circling, Homeland Security throws her a high-paying, short-term contract even the Zero Dogs can't screw up: destroy a capitalist necromancer bent on dominating the gelatin industry with an all-zombie workforce. The catch? She has to take on Special Forces Captain Jake Sanders, a man who threatens both the existence of the team and Andrea's deliberate avoidance of romantic entanglements.

As Andrea strains to hold her dysfunctional team together long enough to derail the corporate zombie apocalypse, the prospect of getting her heart run over by a tank tread is the least of her worries. The government never does anything without an ulterior motive. Jake could be the key to success...or just another bad day at the office for the Zeroes.

Warning: Contains explicit language, intense action and violence, rampaging zombie hordes, a heroine with an attitude and flamethrower, Special Forces commandos, ninjas, apocalyptic necromancer capitalist machinations, absurd parody and mayhem, self-deluded humor, irreverence, geek humor, mutant cats, low-brow comedy, and banana-kiwi-flavored gelatin.

Available now in ebook from Samhain Publishing.

Some secrets are dangerous. This Secret is deadly.

Something Secret This Way Comes
© *2011 Sierra Dean*
Secret McQueen, Book 1

For Secret McQueen, her life feels like the punch line for a terrible joke. Abandoned at birth by her werewolf mother, hired as a teen by the vampire council of New York City to kill rogues, Secret is a part of both worlds, but belongs to neither. At twenty-two, she has carved out as close to a normal life as a bounty hunter can.

When an enemy from her past returns with her death on his mind, she is forced to call on every ounce of her mixed heritage to save herself—and everyone else in the city she calls home. As if the fate of the world wasn't enough to deal with, there's Lucas Rain, King of the East Coast werewolves, who seems to believe he and Secret are fated to be together. Too bad Secret also feels a connection with Desmond, Lucas's second-in-command...

Warning: This book contains a sarcastic, kick-ass bounty hunter; a metaphysical love triangle with two sexy werewolves; a demanding vampire council; and a spicy seasoning of sex and violence.

Available now in ebook and print from Samhain Publishing.

SAMHAIN
PUBLISHING

www.samhainpublishing.com

Green for the planet.
Great for your wallet.

CPSIA information can be obtained at www.ICGtesting.com
Printed in the USA
BVOW021315090412

287209BV00009B/6/P